WICKED FLIRT

KYLIE GILMORE

Cover design by Sweet 'N Spicy Designs

Published by: Extra Fancy Books

ISBN-13: 978-1-942238-41-6

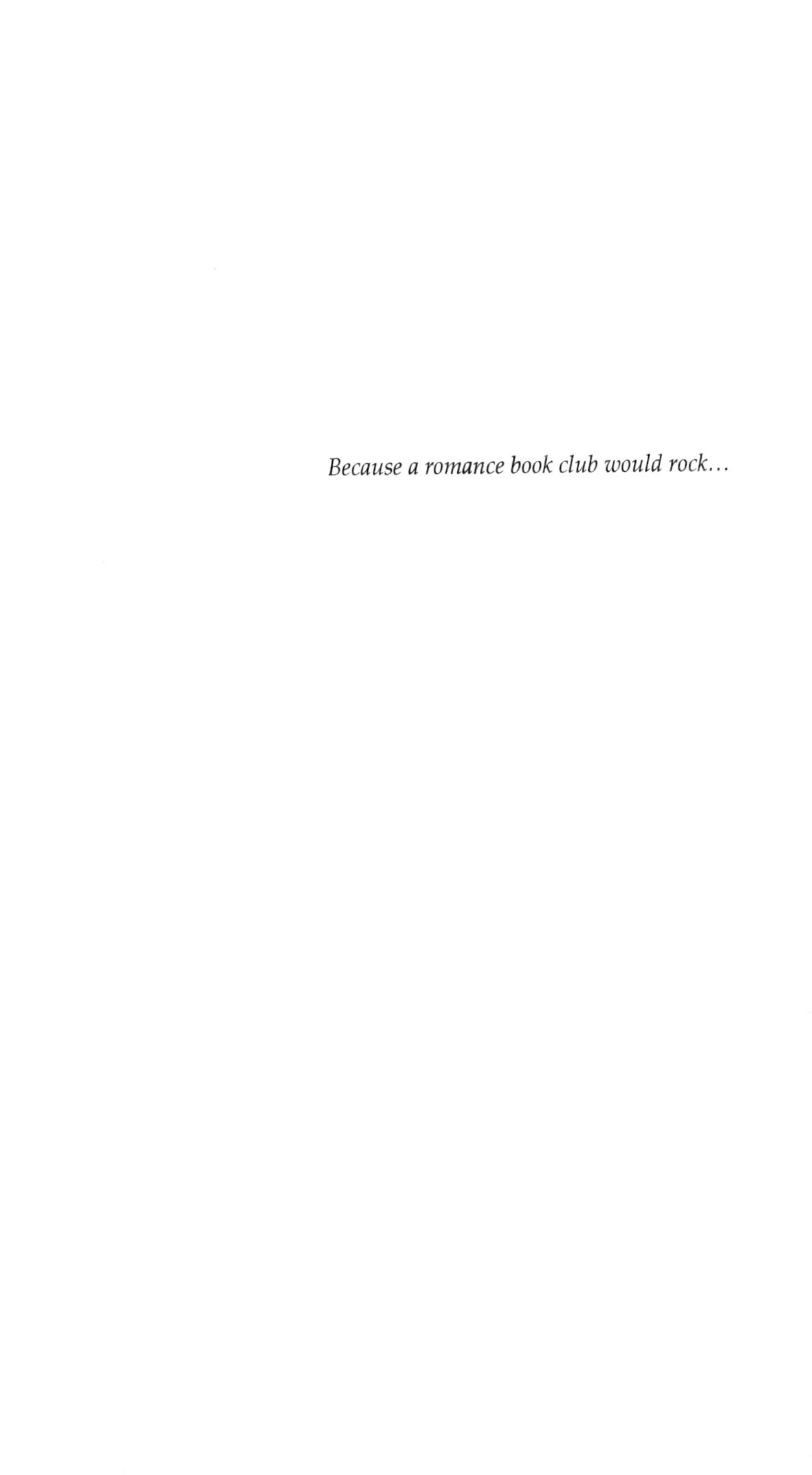

Because a romance book club would rock...

1
———

Lexi Judson had reached her limit of lovey-dovey couples. The only reason she'd shown up for the Clover Park Valentine's Day dance was because her friend Sabrina wanted her there for her big proposal to Logan Campbell. It had turned into a double proposal—Sabrina and Logan had surprised each other with rings, proposing at the same time. Yay for romance and all that crap.

She blew out a breath. She couldn't bail until she was sure she'd introduced herself to everyone she didn't know and, if it seemed appropriate, share that she was now a freelance event planner. So far no good leads. She'd been happy as a corporate event planner at Victoria's Events in New York City, and the news that the small company was closing down for good had been a shock. Victoria's fiancé had gotten an unexpected job opportunity in Paris, and they were leaving in two weeks. *Boom*. Victoria's Events was no more. And did Victoria think about what that would mean for the rest of them being suddenly unemployed? No! She just followed her heart, shut down the office, and screw everyone else.

Lexi had immediately started a massive and desperate job search. No one was hiring. Her severance pay and paltry savings were enough to get her through two months at the most, if she was really frugal. She would *not* be moving back in with her parents or any of her friends. She couldn't deal with being an interloper in one of her friends' love nests.

So here I am, networking at a Valentine's Day dance, as you do.

She scanned the room, quickly skipping over the slow-dancing couples on the dance floor, her eye catching on Marcus Shepard, one of the honorary brothers glued to the Campbell family. The worst one. He was leaning down, smiling and flirting with a young blonde, who looked enthralled. He was a wicked flirt and, if the rumors were true, the lying sort of player who told women he was monogamous when he wasn't. She *despised* cheaters. Men like that always let you down. Like her dad and her older brother and her stupid ex.

She turned away, caught the eager gaze of Sabrina's drunk uncle, a close talker who kept accidentally spitting in her face, and quickly headed toward the bar. Garner's Sports Bar & Grill had catered the event, and Josh Campbell was behind the bar as usual.

"Hey, Lexi, what can I get you?" He didn't add his usual charming smile, probably because he'd had a run-in with her friend Hailey earlier, who was his number one frenemy. The pair were frenemies to the death (or bed, whichever came first) and, equally as juicy, their parents, Joe and Brandy, were currently dating. Joe Campbell was Josh's dad; Brandy Adams was Hailey's mom. Maybe soon Joe and Brandy would get serious and send Hailey in a tailspin, which would make her ripe for the Josh picking. *Muah-ha-ha.*

"Just water, thanks." She'd had her fill of champagne and spiked punch earlier and knew she'd be driving home soon.

He served it up quick.

"Thanks." She took a sip of water. "Any chance you might need an event planned for St. Patrick's Day at Garner's? I'm a freelance event planner now."

He shook his head. "We do the same thing every year with the green beer and the Irish menu. To be honest, there's no room in the budget for an event planner. I'll keep an ear out for you though."

She tried to keep the disappointment from her voice. "No

problem. Thanks." It had been a long shot. She hadn't really expected him or any of her friends to need her services.

Josh gestured to the other side of the room. "Try Marcus. The Burrow is doing really well. He gets all the Wall Street big spenders in there, so if you do an event for him, it might even lead to more work for the Wall Street crowd."

The hair on the back of her neck stood on end. She knew his bar, The Burrow, since she'd been there a few times for parties. It was cool. Still, did she want to work for Marcus, the legendary player? She turned and spotted him flirting with another beautiful woman, this time a brunette, who kept giggling. He smiled at the woman, held up a finger, and pulled his phone from his pocket. His head turned toward her, and he lifted a finger like *just a moment.*

Me? She looked behind her to Josh.

Josh shoved his phone in his pocket. "I texted him. He's coming over."

She gulped. Okay, this was not a problem. She was immune to players. Except she had a type, big muscular men, and Marcus was a prime specimen—tall and wide with huge muscles, a real hulk of a man. This was exactly why she'd kept her distance, so she wouldn't be tempted.

She stepped away from the bar to a nearby quiet corner and girded her loins. *Be polite. No, be professional. And pretend you don't care that he's hit on every single woman here.* They'd met before a few times at parties, where he'd hit on all of her friends. Not her, though, never her. Like she cared. She would've shot him down in a hot second. Really! *Professional in three, two, one…*

Marcus went straight to Josh, who told him something and then gestured over to her.

She lifted a hand with a small smile.

Marcus strode toward her, and she steeled herself for impact.

He stopped in front of her and gave her a half-smile that said *I'm sexy and you know it.* Too bad he was a cheater because he was incredibly nice to look at. His nose had a slight bump at the bridge like it had been broken, but other than that he was exquisite perfection—thick black hair, dark eyes with a fringe of lashes women would kill for, chiseled cheekbones, square jaw with a shadow of dark stubble, and a smoking hot body.

"Hey, Lexi, Josh said you wanted to talk to me about something."

Her mouth went dry. She bobbed her head and took a sip of water. "Yes. Hi. I'm a freelance event planner now and wondered if you might need an event planned for your bar. Maybe for St. Patrick's Day?"

"Got that locked down with a local pub crawl and live band."

Her shoulders drooped. She'd been getting shot down all night. Screw it. She hadn't even wanted to ask him in the first place. He was everything she despised in a man—a lying cheater—and she hadn't wanted to work for him anyway. *Can you really afford to be picky? No job plus no clients plus dwindling bank account equal desperate times.*

She looked up at him. Geez, he must be at least six feet four, a good foot taller than her. She worked for her most pleasant professional tone. "Okay, well, keep me in mind if you ever do need an event planned." She fished her new business card out of her purse and handed it to him.

He slid it into his pocket. "Sure," he said flatly.

It was clear he didn't need her services. She squared her shoulders and drained her water. She was *done*. She'd put in her time, already congratulated the happy couple, and now she could finally bail.

She jumped. Someone just pinched her ass! She turned, face-to-face again with drunk Uncle Spitty. She'd forgotten his real name.

He leered at her. "There you are, girl! Let's go to my place for a nightcap." Apparently he'd forgotten her name too.

"Don't touch me again," she bit out.

Marcus's arm dropped over her shoulders. "She's with me and we're about to leave."

She froze, shocked at Marcus's gentlemanly move saving her from Uncle Spitty.

Uncle Spitty leaned close. "What about us?" Spittle sprinkled her cheek. *Gross.* She was about to back up a step when Marcus used his grip on her shoulder to turn her away, guiding her toward the exit.

She didn't appreciate the manhandling, but what the hell. She'd wanted to leave anyway.

"Don't go!" Uncle Spitty hollered belatedly.

She took a few steps away with Marcus before glancing over her shoulder. Uncle Spitty was making his unsteady way to the bar.

She halted in her tracks, and Marcus stopped too, looking down at her in question. Like he was waiting to follow her lead. Curious. She'd figured him for the *large and in charge* kind of guy. "Thanks for calling off Uncle Spitty. I got it from here."

Marcus dropped his big hand from her shoulder. "No problem. Uncle Spitty?"

She nodded. "He's a close talker. He's been accidentally spitting on me all night."

He laughed, a rich deep rumble of a laugh.

She laughed too. This whole night had been ridiculous—networking in a room teeming with love-goggled couples, fleeing Uncle Spitty's close conversations, pretending she was enjoying the heck out of the romantic night flying solo.

"Hey, Lexi! Hey, Marcus!"

Crap. Her friend Hailey approached, wearing a deep red off-the-shoulder dress with red ballet flats in honor of Valentine's Day. Little Rose's white furry head peeked out of Hailey's pink doggie purse. She really hoped Hailey wasn't about to do some matchmaking. Lexi had been very firm with Hailey about the matchmaking, but it was no use. Lexi was the last single woman in their formerly all singles Happy Endings Book Club, a romance book club that Hailey had started with the goal of helping every last one of them find their very own happy ending. Lexi had only joined the book club because two of her friends were members. Now she had a big ol' bull's-eye on her forehead with a perky strawberry blond hunter closing in. Hailey was also single, but that didn't count. Hailey was in a relationship with her dog.

Marcus poured on the charm for Hailey, saying in a deep honey voice, "Hey, sweetheart, how's it going?"

Hailey sped up. "Great!" Her pale blue eyes were huge, taking them both in. Rose's big dark eyes seemed equally surprised. Rose had a pink bow with red hearts on her white tuft of a ponytail perched right in the center of her head. The bow matched her dog sweater. *Give the poor dog some dignity.* "I just need to borrow Lexi for a minute."

Next thing she knew, Hailey had dragged her several feet away. Lexi braced herself for the third degree leading to some serious Marcus matchmaking—nail that guy down—but Hailey surprised her.

"What're you doing with Marcus?" Hailey whispered. "Are you guys together? Rumor has it, he's a player."

Lexi glanced over at Marcus, standing a distance away, waiting for her. Maybe to shield her from Uncle Spitty? She turned back to Hailey. "We're not together. He just helped me avoid a drunk guy."

Hailey squeezed Lexi's arm, looking relieved. "Don't get me wrong, he's a good guy, he's just not someone you want to get involved with."

Obviously Hailey meant well. She was a good friend. It was just that she'd stepped one too many times into aggressive territory with the matchmaking. "Thanks for having my back, girl." She gave her a fist bump, which Hailey returned. "Have a good night."

"You too." Hailey smiled, waved goodbye to Marcus, and headed back to the dance.

Lexi headed for the door, and Marcus kept pace with her. "I was on my way out too," he said, reaching for the door handle and holding it open for her.

"Thanks," she mumbled, walking out to the small foyer.

She pulled her black wool coat off the rack and stuck her arm in the sleeve. Marcus shifted behind her and helped her put it on.

"Uh, thanks," she said softly, feeling a little weird in a

good way. No guy had ever helped her on with her coat before. What did it say about her that her expectations with men were so low that she delighted in such a simple gesture? It shouldn't be such a big deal that he had good manners. Probably Mr. Campbell had drilled them into his head just like all the Campbell guys and their honorary brothers.

He snagged his black wool coat and shrugged his bulky shoulders into it. They matched in black coats. They were also alone in the small space, which suddenly felt filled with large man.

Marcus buttoned his coat, glad to be done with tonight. He'd put on his game face, smiling and flirting like usual, but his heart wasn't in it. All he had to do was look at the dance floor, where all of his friends were stupid-happy with their women, even tough hard-ass Ethan had found someone who adored him and only him, and his mood plummeted. He felt like a lone lion hungry for a satisfying meal. The women he flirted with tonight were too young or too dopey or too into partying.

He glanced at Lexi. She was also a hard no, a prickly man-hater from what he'd seen, more likely to bite his head off than flirt back, which was why he'd never bothered flirting with her before. Up close her brown almond-shaped eyes gleamed with intelligence. Her sleek dark brown hair was up in a twist, her light tan skin smooth, her smile, when it appeared, was slightly devious. That was who she reminded him of—the love of his life, Bitty. Sleek and soft with sharp claws. He still missed that cat.

Lexi's skintight dark blue dress—low cut, ending mid-thigh—had caught his eye earlier. Any man would appreciate a beautiful woman showing a lot of skin. Didn't mean he wanted a relationship with her. He was looking for a woman who adored him. He figured if Ethan could manage it, then Marcus could too. A prickly man-hater did *not* fit the bill. She was the last single woman among her friends for a reason.

And it didn't count that he was practically the last of the bachelors among his friends. He had relationship *intentions.* He'd just been too busy to do anything about it between work and his mom's illness.

He stiffened, pulling his phone from his pocket. He'd set it to vibrate. It was a text from his mom asking him to please bring the groceries tonight. It was Friday, and usually he did the grocery shopping for her on Sunday. He exhaled sharply, her current condition weighing heavily on his shoulders. Ever since she'd lost her job just before Christmas, she hadn't left the house. Not even to go to dinner with him at their favorite diner. Agoraphobia, it was called. He'd felt better when he'd discovered it had a name, which meant other people had been through similar stuff and had come out the other side. So far he hadn't had any luck getting her to talk to a professional about it.

He texted back. *I'm at a Valentine's Day dance. I'll stop by with the groceries after.*

Three dots blinked on the phone screen as she typed. He waited, brows furrowed with concern.

"Everything okay?" Lexi asked gently.

His head jerked up, surprised she actually sounded like she cared. He must look as worried as he felt. "My mom's not well." He glanced down at his phone.

Mom: *Thank you. I hope you meet a nice girl there. It makes me so sad to see you alone.*

Sure, he was alone on Valentine's Day surrounded by his whipped lovesick friends, but that didn't mean...He swallowed hard. There was a quiet dignity in being alone. He'd read that somewhere. His mom had been on him for years to settle down. He was thirty-three, not old, and he'd already been settled down once, but lately she'd been saying she needed to know he had someone because she wouldn't always be around. She wasn't suicidal, she just felt old at fifty-one, which he didn't think was very old at all. She had plenty of good years ahead of her if only he could get her past her fear of leaving the house.

He slowly lifted his gaze to Lexi, also looking very alone,

and had a crazy thought. What if he brought Lexi with him to his mom's house? He'd do anything to make his mom happy. It killed him to see her reduced to a shadow of her former self.

"Sorry to hear about your mom," Lexi said. "What kind of illness does she have?"

His throat tightened unexpectedly at her concern. He'd been the man of the house since he was seven years old. It had always been him and his mom against the world. But he was blowing it. Her condition was getting worse, and he was worried enough that he found himself blurting the truth. "It's not a physical illness, more mental. She was laid off right before Christmas and hasn't left her house since. Almost two months."

"My aunt had that. Agoraphobia."

His jaw dropped. "Really? Did she get better?"

Lexi nodded. "Eventually. My mom and I spent a lot of time with her, being supportive and encouraging. She worked with a psychiatrist too. She's a lot better now and goes out regularly."

Hope speared through him. Lexi might be able to do a lot more than just brighten his mom's day by posing as his girl-friend, she might be able to help her with the agoraphobia. Maybe Lexi could tell her about her aunt and how well she was doing now. Maybe his mom would finally be willing to talk to a professional.

"Lexi, I've got a proposition for you."

Her eyes widened. "Uh, thanks, but—"

"I'll hire you to do an event for my bar. You could do Fat Tuesday for Mardi Gras and, in return, you show up with me a few times at my mom's place."

She stared at him. "I'd love to do an event, but you, uh, really want me to meet your mom? We barely know each other."

"I think your experience with your aunt could help her. But I know you'll need to get on her good side, which is why…we'd pretend you were my serious girlfriend. Just for a while. Maybe eight weeks." He pressed his lips tightly together. "I *really* hope she's doing better by then."

Lexi remained quiet, so he barreled on. "It's been tough dealing with it long distance. I'm in the city; she's here in Eastman. Anyway, she needs me to do the grocery shopping. We could do a quick grocery run, drop them off, I'll introduce you as my girlfriend, and then I'll tell her we have Valentine's Day plans and need to go."

She studied him. He waited impatiently. Now that he had a glimmer of hope, he wanted to act on it right now. He knew this first visit would be too soon to mention Lexi's aunt. His mom had to be eased into it, which meant they needed to get the ball rolling now with an introduction.

"Okay," she finally said, her lips set in a grim line. "I could really use the work. I lost my job a few days ago, and it's tough to get a freelance business started." She held up a finger. "But there has to be rules. Let's make it six weeks and no funny business."

The tension drained from him, making him feel lighter and downright cheerful. He walked ahead of Lexi and held the outside door open for her. "No problem. I'm not very funny."

She brushed past him, and he caught her citrusy scent. "Sex is off the table."

He grinned and followed her out the door. "Like you're my type."

She glared at him and he laughed, dropping a hand on her head and mussing her hair, completely screwing up her updo. He had a "little sister," Mad, and knew just how to make her crazy. Women hated when you messed up their hair.

He smirked, watching Lexi attempt to salvage her hairstyle. "You'll be like Mad, my honorary little sister, trailing me around and looking up at me adoringly."

She gave up on her former hairstyle and pulled the pins from her shoulder-length hair, shaking it out. It settled in place like silk. He stopped smirking and quickly strode ahead of her through the parking lot, opening the passenger-side door of his red Audi.

She got into his car and looked up at him. "You treat your little sister nice," she teased.

He gave her a small smile. "Joe Campbell's influence. He taught me to treat women like I'd want someone to treat my little sister, with care and respect."

"Then I should thank Joe. What a guy!"

He inclined his head before shutting the door. This would be easy—a pretend girlfriend to make his mom feel better without any of the headache and work of keeping a woman happy. A mutually agreeable deal that solved both of their problems. What could go wrong?

2

———

Marcus made quick work of the grocery shopping. His mom had texted him a list. Lexi took one look at it and efficiently scoured the produce section, saving him loads of time. He hadn't introduced a woman to his mom since his ex-wife, but these were desperate times. He was her only kid, and his dad had died when Marcus was seven, shortly after being arrested on drug charges. In exchange for a more lenient jail sentence, his dad had snitched on the drug kingpin he worked for. He'd been killed while out on bail, awaiting his trial. Marcus's mom had said all his dad had wanted was to get back home to them. To Marcus's young ears, it sounded like if it weren't for him, his dad would've lived. A heavy load for a seven-year-old.

He'd witnessed his mom's crying many nights after that and resolved that he had to take care of her. They were more like friends than parent and kid since she'd practically been a kid when she had him, only eighteen. Growing up, it seemed his mom was doing better, until he'd witnessed her first panic attack when he was thirteen. He'd thought she was going to die, her heart racing, her breathing shallow. He'd called an ambulance and got her to the ER. Later, he found out she'd been having panic attacks for years. No matter how much he'd tried to take care of her, his love hadn't been enough.

And now she was worse with the agoraphobia. Maybe his love would never be enough for his mom. Maybe what he needed was to bring in backup. In this case, Lexi. He couldn't believe his luck in finding someone who understood his mom's condition and actually knew what to do. Lexi might be a prickly man-hater, but she was great with women. Just look at all her close friends and how she'd helped her aunt get better. And, if he was being honest, she'd become a lot less prickly after he'd told her the deal with his mom.

He met up with Lexi at the register and paid for everything.

"Anything else I should know about your mom?" she asked once they were in the car.

"Her name is Lia. She used to be a secretary. She's sweet. Soft-spoken, gentle."

"Okay, so kinda like Sabrina." Their mutual friend Sabrina was a relationship counselor.

"My mom's not as good with all the feelings stuff as Sabrina, but, yeah, sweet like that."

They drove for a few minutes in silence, his mind on his mom. It alarmed him to see her just sitting on the sofa day after day. She did crossword puzzles, watched TV, some reading, but she had no connection to the outside world. Even her friends from her old job had given up on her, and she'd been there for twenty years. Now it was up to him. As long as he didn't push her, she seemed fine. But the minute he brought up talking to a professional or even just taking a walk with him, she got nervous, her hands fluttering in the air, stepping closer to her bedroom, her sanctuary.

He pulled into the driveway of the ranch home he'd bought her a few years back. It was the first house she'd ever lived in—after years of apartment living—and she loved it. She had a vegetable garden out back. Maybe when the weather warmed up, she'd venture to the backyard for some gardening.

He popped the trunk, gathered the grocery bags, and headed to the front door. Lexi followed and stood next to him on the small concrete porch, looking a little nervous.

"Just play it cool," he told her. "Follow my lead." He pressed the doorbell and waited. He'd texted his mom at the supermarket, telling her he was on his way, so she knew it was him.

He heard the slide of the chain lock, the deadbolt, and then his mom slowly opened the door. She was petite, a little shorter than Lexi, and wearing her green fleece robe over pajamas. It was a little after nine at night, but that wasn't why she was in a robe and pajamas. She never bothered getting dressed anymore, like that took away the possibility of leaving the house. She did a double take when she saw Lexi, her brown eyes huge with surprise.

"Mom, I brought Lexi since we're celebrating Valentine's Day together."

"Hi!" Lexi said brightly. "Nice to meet you."

His mom smoothed her dark brown jaw-length hair and gathered her robe tighter around her. "Hi," she said softly before shooting him a dark look. "You didn't mention you were bringing company. I haven't prepared."

He lifted all the bags in both hands. "I brought everything you need. We won't be staying long. We have to get back to our Valentine's Day."

His mom backed up, letting them in. "Of course. Thank you for taking the time to pick up my groceries. You said you'd be in town, so..." She pressed her lips together. "I'm sorry for interrupting your special night."

He headed to the kitchen, both women trailing him. "It's fine. I wanted you to meet Lexi anyway." He set the bags down on the counter. "Lexi, this is the amazing Lia Shepard, queen of the paella." His mom had been born here, but her family was originally from Spain.

His mom blushed. "Marcus!" She turned to Lexi. "He exaggerates. He'll eat anything."

"I love paella," Lexi said, taking off her coat.

"That's a beautiful dress," his mom said. "I'm so embarrassed you caught me in my robe."

"No big," Lexi said. "I'm a pretty casual person."

"Would you like a drink?" his mom asked Lexi. "I have

water or milk." At least he didn't have to worry about his mom drinking. She'd always lived clean, even though his dad saw no problem with occasionally sampling the drugs he sold.

"Water would be nice," Lexi said, taking a seat at the small round kitchen table, her coat draped across her lap. A white tablecloth hand-embroidered with a colorful chain of flowers covered the table. His mom liked pretty things and was handy at a lot of domestic stuff. She'd always been a home-body, but never to this extreme.

His mom bustled to the cabinet and then the sink, getting Lexi's water before joining her at the table.

He unpacked the bags and started putting the food away, one ear cocked to his mom and Lexi's conversation.

"So how did you meet Marcus?" his mom asked.

Lexi replied in a very convincing voice. "We have a lot of the same friends, so you know how these things go. We met a few times, he was a flirty charmer, and then finally we sorta connected."

He smiled to himself. That actually sounded like it could've happened. He *was* a flirty charmer.

"Have you been dating long?" his mom asked eagerly.

"How long's it been, babe?" Lexi asked him.

Way to pass the buck. "One-month anniversary coming up tomorrow," he said, not looking at either of them. His mom could read a lie in his eyes. It was a harmless white lie for the greater good. He shouldn't feel so guilty.

"Do you live here or in the city?" his mom asked Lexi. "What kind of work do you do? Do you have family nearby?"

The rush of questions was a good sign. His mom hadn't shown much interest in anything in a long while. He hoped Lexi didn't mind. He glanced over at her.

"I'm a corporate event planner," Lexi said with a smile. "I live nearby in Clover Park and commute into the city for work. My parents live about forty-five minutes away. My older brother's an hour away with his wife. Everyone's still in Connecticut."

"That's so nice," his mom said enthusiastically.

He relaxed. This was going even better than he'd hoped.

Lexi nodded and then got serious. "Marcus told me you lost your job recently. I know how hard that is. I recently lost mine too. Have you had any leads for something new?"

Marcus stiffened. That was too forward. Shit. He should've briefed Lexi on easing into things with his mom. Even he couldn't get that kind of information out of her. It wasn't clear if his mom had given up looking for a job or had just faced a lot of rejection. For a while, he'd been emailing her job listings, but she'd stopped checking her email.

His mom's voice was high and reedy. "It seems Marcus has shared a lot about me and told me very little about you."

He turned, shot Lexi a look that said *cool it*, and told his mom, "Lexi's way into me, which means she wanted to know all about my life. You're a big part of that."

His mom frowned, still not happy with his sharing.

Lexi chimed in. "I did ask him a bunch of questions. Actually, my aunt had a similar issue as you with the agoraphobia and—"

"Phobia!" His mom's hand went to her throat. "I don't have a phobia."

Marcus winced.

"My friend Sabrina is a counselor," Lexi said, seeming oblivious to his mom's agitation. "We should bring her by to meet you. Maybe she'd have some tips to help with your current trouble."

"What trouble?" his mom asked, turning wide panicky eyes to him. "Marcus?"

"Not trouble, really," he said. "I just mentioned you haven't been going out as much. Maybe Lexi thought having a counselor who made a house visit could be good."

"I don't need counseling," his mom said, standing abruptly. "I'm fine." Her hands fluttered in the air and her eyes darted around the room. "I just need to work again. That's all." She backed up a step.

"Mom, it's okay."

"I misunderstood," Lexi said in a soothing voice.

"You don't know me," his mom told Lexi in a voice that shook with her agitation. "How dare you come here and say all these awful things!" She turned and fled the room, probably going back to her bedroom sanctuary.

He rubbed his temple.

Lexi stood. "I'll go apologize. I didn't mean to overstep."

He shook his head. "I'll deal with it."

"Tell her I'm sorry, okay? I only wanted to help."

He nodded once, quickly tucked the food into cabinets and the refrigerator, took a deep breath, and headed for his mom's room.

He knocked. No reply. "Mom, it's me. I wanted to say goodbye."

"Come in."

He opened the door. She was sitting up against the headboard with the TV on at a low volume. She grabbed the remote and muted it.

"Close the door behind you," she said.

He did and walked over to her side. "Sorry if Lexi crossed the line. She meant well. She feels bad and asked me to apologize for her. I didn't think you'd want her in here."

"I don't like her. She's coarse, no sensitivity. You don't just walk into someone's home unannounced and then act judgmental, doling out advice. Obviously she doesn't respect her elders—"

"Mom, you're not elderly at all."

His mom's fingers tightened in the blanket. "I am her elder and she treated me disrespectfully. I don't want you to see her anymore, is that clear? And she's not welcome in my home."

He scrubbed a hand over his face. He definitely should've prepped Lexi better. This was supposed to be step one in helping his mom. Now it was blown out of the water. What hope did he have of helping her on his own? She wouldn't listen to him. He had no idea what to do next.

His mom grabbed his hand with icy fingers. "Swear you won't see her anymore."

She was in a fragile state and he didn't want to upset her any further. "I swear." He gave her hand a squeeze. "Text or call if you need anything else."

She tucked herself under the covers, pulling them up to her chin. "Thank you, Marcus."

He headed out, the burden heavy on his shoulders once again. Just before he went through the doorway, he muttered sarcastically under his breath, "We're getting married next week."

"Over my dead body," his mom called. The woman had super hearing.

That went well. Not.

He found Lexi standing in the living room, her coat already on. He inclined his head toward the door. "Let's go."

The moment they were outside, Lexi asked, "Did you tell her I was sorry? Is she still mad at me?"

He couldn't tell her she was banished from his mom's house and his life forever, so he hedged a bit. "She's just really sensitive."

"I feel terrible."

"Sorry I brought you into this." Failure was not an option, but he was running out of options. He opened the car door for her and shut it behind her.

Once they were back on the street, Lexi said, "You really should get Sabrina over here. She could get her started with some individual counseling. I'm sure she'd be willing to make a house call. And then, at some point, your mom could see a professional in an office."

He clenched his jaw. "Don't you get it? She hated that idea. Didn't you notice how worked up she got at the suggestion?"

"Has she met Sabrina?"

"No."

"So she has no idea how easy it is to talk to her. Don't you find just being near Sabrina is relaxing? She's always so calm and composed, her voice nice and even. A steady sort."

He shook his head. "She's not ready. If I push too hard, it's only going to make it worse."

She was quiet for a moment.

He gripped the steering wheel. "Look, it's not your problem."

"But I want to help. Agoraphobia is so limiting. What about a therapy dog? Hailey might be able to get one through the trainer she used for Rose."

He stopped at a red light and turned to her. "That might actually be a good idea. She'd be focused on taking care of the dog. Maybe she'd even start taking it for walks."

"Yeah, and she has a fenced-in yard, so it wouldn't be high pressure. She could let it run around the yard until she was ready to venture a little farther."

He smiled, really pleased with this new idea. He'd been so stuck on how to fix the situation. Lexi had screwed up, but her heart was in the right place. "Ya know, I swore to my mom I'd stop seeing you, but you're not so bad."

Her jaw dropped. "Oh my God, she made you swear? She must really hate me. Marcus, I have to go back there and fix this."

"No, you don't. You gave me a workable solution. That's all I need."

She wrung her hands together. "I feel awful."

The light turned green and he hit the accelerator. "You're off the hook. I'll tell her we broke up next time I see her."

"What a disaster," Lexi muttered. "Major fake-girlfriend fail."

"I'll say."

"Thanks."

He shook his head at how badly it had gone down.

She twirled a lock of her hair. "How come your mom doesn't have anyone? Your dad's not around? No family? No friends?"

He was surprised she cared enough to ask after his mom had dismissed her. "Her friends gave up after a while. She wouldn't call them back or ever show up to anything. And I'm her only family besides my grandparents, but they don't live nearby. No brothers or sisters, and my dad died when I was seven." His mom had insisted he not bother her parents, who were enjoying their long-overdue retirement in Florida.

Not for the first time he wondered how his mom's life would've been different if his dad had lived. Maybe she wouldn't have had any issues at all. She'd loved Marcus's dad, and Marcus had too. His dad hadn't been a violent man, just a hustler, looking for easy money. A charmer, his mom had always said. Guess the apple didn't fall far from the tree.

"I'm sorry," Lexi said gently. "It's hard on you."

He swallowed over the lump in his throat, surprised once again by Lexi. She'd seen through his cheerful facade at his mom's place to his real anguish. His whole life he'd tried to help his mom, and she just got worse and worse, from crying to panic attacks to agoraphobia. His love was not enough.

His love hadn't been enough for his wife either. They'd divorced four years ago. A disaster of a relationship—betrayal, cheating, lying.

Maybe his love would never be enough for anyone. Maybe he'd never be enough.

"Marcus, are you okay?"

He snapped to attention, pushing down the dark thoughts. "It's nothing she wouldn't do for me if our situations were reversed. It's always been the two of us against the world."

"That's *really* hard on a kid."

His mom had done the best she could. His protective instincts made his voice come out harsh. "I'm thirty-three years old, a grown-ass man who's got his shit together. That means I look after her."

She got quiet.

Now he felt bad. Lexi was only trying to be a friend. "Too harsh?" he asked.

"No. It was actually perfect. I like a grown-ass man who's got his shit together much better than a charming flirt."

"Yeah?"

"Yeah."

"Huh." That had not been his experience with women. Flirting usually went a long way.

She fidgeted a bit in her seat and gave him a small smile before turning her head away, looking out the window.

She didn't seem like such a man-hater now. She was a little insensitive, but also straightforward. No BS with her. No games. Just straight-up truth. Damn, she was starting to grow on him.

3
———

Lexi wasn't eye-fucking a sweaty, insanely muscular Marcus in a loose white tank top and black athletic pants any more than her friends Sabrina and Ally were, so it was just normal woman behavior.

They were at Sabrina's apartment on Sunday, helping her with the move to her fiancé, Logan's house. The women were packing Sabrina's dishes and related crap in the kitchen while the men—Marcus, Logan, and Ethan—hauled her furniture out. Logan had a muscular athletic build, and Ethan, Ally's fiancé, was in tiptop shape as a cop. Still, Marcus's muscles were so massive she'd bet he could carry the sofa he was currently helping move all by himself.

"Turn it sideways," Marcus told Logan.

Logan had just reached the propped-open front door with his end of the sofa. He angled it, and the sofa fit, the two of them heading through the doorway. Ethan followed behind carrying the coffee table.

Sabrina headed for the living room, bending to pick up something from the carpet where the sofa had just been. Her long dirty blond hair was up in a ponytail. She looked up at them, her brown eyes bright, her round cheeks glowing, probably from a morning fuck with Logan. She'd been pretty open that Logan couldn't keep his hands off her and vice versa. "You guys! Look what I found! Remember?"

Lexi squinted at something little and brown. *Err…*

Sabrina joined Lexi and Ally in the kitchen. "It's from last year's Super Bowl party." It was a little plastic football on a stick. Sabrina had stuck a bunch of them in a chocolate cake that she'd decorated to look like a football field. She was too much of a foodie to actually dye the chocolate icing green, so she'd used small amounts of green piping around the edges. Sabrina was truly a domestic goddess, and Lexi had been totally spoiled, popping into Sabrina's apartment down the hall and snarfing down homemade meals and desserts. Lexi was really going to miss her. Her throat closed. This sucked.

"That was a fun night," Lexi said, her voice cracking. She cleared her throat. "I can't believe you guys are leaving me here all by my lonesome." It had been so nice for a while there with Ally, Sabrina, and Missy all living down the hall from her. Almost like a college dorm, popping into each other's apartments whenever. Now Ally lived with Ethan, Missy lived with her fiancé, Ben—the two of them currently on a romantic getaway in Aruba—and Sabrina was moving in with Logan.

Sabrina hugged her. "Aww, Lexi, we'll visit."

"I miss you guys too," Ally said, shoving her blond bangs out of her eyes. "It's not the same now that we don't live down the hall from each other." She gave Lexi's arm a squeeze. "It does kinda suck to be the last one here."

Ethan returned and gave Ally a wink. He had short dirty blond hair and blue eyes, the same coloring as Ally, except their personalities were complete opposites. Ethan was a tough guy who rarely smiled, and Ally was bubbly and easily excitable. Ally beamed at him like he was a sex god wrapped in chocolate.

Lexi blew out a breath. Ya know, fucking couples and their sappy happiness all *in your face*. Not that she begrudged her friends' happiness. It was just that it wasn't the same between them anymore. It was all "let me check in with Ethan" or "I'll see if Logan can come too."

Lexi went back to packing Sabrina's coffee mugs.

Sabrina leaned against the counter next to Lexi. "What's the deal with you and Marcus? He keeps looking over at you, and you've definitely been checking him out."

Lexi sucked in air. He was checking her out too? She hadn't realized. A warm tingling spread over her skin.

Ally closed a cabinet and turned to Lexi. "Yeah, how long's this been going on? I saw you two at the Valentine's dance flirting up a storm."

Ethan rushed out of the apartment with an end table, probably not comfortable with girl talk.

"We weren't flirting," Lexi said. "He helped me avoid a drunk guy." She didn't mention it was Sabrina's uncle, not wanting her to feel bad.

"I saw you leave the dance with him," Ally said. "Spill." Her friends didn't miss much.

She couldn't share about her deal with Marcus from two days ago both because it was now off and he might want his mom's issue to be kept private. She'd felt so bad about messing up with his mom that she'd told Marcus not to worry about the event he'd offered in exchange. He still wanted to help her out, but she just didn't feel right about it.

Lexi lifted one shoulder. "We just happened to be leaving the dance at the same time. Now you're all caught up." She hadn't talked to Marcus since that night, which wasn't unusual. They didn't know each other very well. She didn't even have his number. He had hers from her business card, though. Not that she'd really expected anything. It was just that he was so sweet with his mom, she felt like she'd caught a glimpse of a different Marcus.

Sabrina nodded. "That's good. He can't seem to stay with just one woman. Logan says Marcus was seeing three women at the same time. Definitely not someone you could expect to have a committed monogamous relationship with. Major red flags on that guy. Not that he's not nice. Logan is close with him, so he must be a good guy, he's just not relationship material."

There you have it, folks! The relationship counselor has made her diagnosis and it's not good!

"Yup," Lexi said. Sabrina wasn't wrong. Marcus *was* a good guy to have as a friend, but not more than that. She'd seen his good side shining through—the way he took care of his mom and the fact that he still wanted to honor his part of the deal even after she'd screwed up her part of the deal as his fake girlfriend. She'd heard the rumor about the three-women-at-the-same-time thing, also had heard he didn't believe in monogamy, and that he left women devastated in his wake, all of them apparently believing they were special when they were just one of many. Obviously he lied to them, cheating on them and letting them think they had something real. Unfortunately, she was intimately familiar with that type of man—her ex, Noah, and his flavor of the week, her dad's affairs and her long-suffering mom crying over it and then forgiving him over and over. Lexi had tried so hard to comfort her mom as a young girl and then, when she was older, begged her mom to move on or at least stand up for herself. And Lexi's older brother was exactly like their father, already cheating on his newly pregnant bride, a sweet woman whom Lexi both liked and felt sorry for.

The reasons not to be with Marcus kept piling up—he was a lying cheater, his mom hated her, and her friends didn't approve. The *no-thanks* trifecta. So why did she feel disappointed? Maybe the rumors about him weren't true. She was having trouble reconciling them with the kindness she'd seen in him.

Ally raised her brows at Sabrina, her blue eyes dancing with mischief. "Maybe Lexi just wants a little fun in a big package." She turned to Lexi. "You want to bang him, right?"

Lexi snorted at the blunt question.

"Ally!" Sabrina exclaimed.

"I'm sorry," Ally said, not sounding sorry at all. "It's just that he sort of oozes sex. Maybe I should've said you would enjoy some early foreplay stuff?"

Lexi burst out laughing.

Logan and Marcus walked back in. "What's so funny?"

Logan asked, already smiling in anticipation. He was a real cutie when he smiled, his brown eyes sparkling with good humor. His light brown beard was hot too.

"Nothing," Sabrina said primly. "Ally said something inappropriate."

Ethan walked into the kitchen, his eyes only for his love. "Ally loves inappropriate."

Ally laughed. "I do. It's terrible."

Ethan cracked a smile, his face lighting up like Ally was the sun and he worshipped her. "It's great."

"What's next?" Marcus asked, hands on his hips, giving them all a peek under his tank top to sculpted pecs and ridged abs. All of him—from his huge shoulders to the round massive bulge of biceps to his chest and abs—glistened with sweat. Testosterone city. "Dining room table?"

All three women stared at him. It was impossible to look away from all that sweaty sexy male.

"Yeah, let's get the chairs first," Logan said.

A few minutes later, the men left with a pair of chairs each.

"Woo!" Ally exclaimed, fanning her face with her hand. "I can see why you've been checking him out so much, Lex! He looks like a male model—ooh, even better—like one of those sexy stripper guys!"

"Just because the man is built," Sabrina said in an even tone, "does *not* make him a stripper."

Lexi flashed to a stripping Marcus, her cheeks flushing, and quickly pushed that image out of her mind. She dropped to her knees to close the flaps on the box she'd been filling, hiding her embarrassing reaction.

Ally pulled some plastic containers from a cabinet. "He's *like* a stripper. I know he owns a bar. Come on, Lexi! It's *us*. You can't tell me you're just going to ignore all that studliness!"

"What do you want me to say?" she asked, holding the box closed and reaching one hand up to the counter for the tape. "Marcus is sex personified. He's a magnificent stud, panty-melting man candy, an orgasm-inducing eye-fuck. And he's a man who's got his shit together. What could be better than that?"

"Thank you," Marcus replied.

Lexi squeaked in surprise, nearly falling over. She shot her friends fierce glares for not warning her he'd returned. Sabrina grimaced apologetically. Ally shrugged and whispered, "He just got here."

She slowly stood to face him, her cheeks flaming. And she was *so* not a blusher.

He stared at her for an excruciatingly awkward moment.

"Girl talk," she said, really hoping he hadn't heard anything before the got-his-shit-together part.

He jerked his chin. "Figured."

Logan and Ethan returned, and Marcus went to help them carry out the dining room table, a smile playing over his lips.

She stood perfectly still, frozen in awkward limbo, waiting for the men to leave. As soon as they cleared the doorway, she turned to her friends. "How much did he hear?"

"I think he got here at orgasm," Ally said matter-of-factly. "But he might've heard more from the hallway. The door's propped open and you were kinda loud."

Sabrina nodded. "Orgasm-inducing eye-fuck. You were on a roll. I think I sort of froze when he did."

Lexi covered her face with both hands. "I don't think I've ever been so embarrassed in my life."

Someone rubbed her back soothingly. Ally. "Be glad if that's the worst of your embarrassment. I've done much more embarrassing things."

Lexi dropped her hands and scowled. "I doubt that."

Ally smiled. "Guess where I was when Ethan and I first connected."

"Your college reunion, right?" Lexi said.

"Yes, but much worse," Ally replied. "It was the men's room at the hotel where they had the reunion. I was hiding in a stall, bawling my eyes out over my ex, and he walked in. I'm standing there hoping he doesn't notice me, and then he comes right up to the stall, identifies himself as a police officer, and asks if I need any help."

That did sound bad. Super embarrassing. She could just imagine tough Ethan ready to come to the rescue in cop mode while Ally was sobbing in the men's room. Tears were private.

"Why—" Lexi started to ask.

"The ladies' room had a line," Ally said, anticipating her question.

Lexi actually did feel a little better hearing that. Embarrassing misery loves company, she supposed. And it had turned out just fine for Ally and Ethan, so she didn't feel bad about enjoying the story.

Sabrina grimaced. "Lex, the reason I warned you off Marcus earlier is because we worked it out this morning for him to stay here for a few months while my lease is still active. Just part-time, Sunday through Wednesday, so he can look in on his mom more. My lease isn't up until June. He was nice enough to offer to pay part of the rent, but Logan already covered it for me."

Lexi's brain froze on "stay here for a few months." She gaped at Sabrina in complete and total shock. "Here? He's living here? In your old apartment? Right down the hall from me?"

"Oh boy, we'd better get her some water," Ally said, looking around for a glass.

"Here, take a seat," Sabrina said, patting a kitchen chair.

Lexi was too shocked to move. Ally and Sabrina pushed her to a kitchen chair, and she flopped down heavily. Her friends were talking to her in soothing tones, but she couldn't focus on them, her brain homing in on the alarming fact of Marcus living down the hall. Her new *magnificent stud, panty-melting man-candy, orgasm-inducing eye-fuck man who's got his shit together* neighbor. The man she knew better than to get involved with yet some part of her was still drawn to him. Resisting Marcus when she lived here and he lived in the city was easy, but right down the hall?

The men returned.

She felt Marcus's eyes on her and caught his concerned

look. "Why're you living here?" she asked, her voice loud and embarrassingly high.

"So I can look in on my mom," he replied. "Problem?"

His mom. He'd uprooted and rearranged his entire schedule to look after her. Major good-guy points. She was in trouble.

She kept her voice calm and composed. "No, I don't have a problem."

"Good."

She couldn't seem to stop talking, even though everyone was watching them curiously. "It's just that I live down the hall, so, uh, I guess we'll be neighbors." *Just shut up.*

He raised a brow and lifted the bottom of his tank top to wipe the sweat from his face. Her gaze dropped to six-pack abs, muscular ridges down his sides, and a dark happy trail leading to a sizable bulge. Her stomach dipped, a low ache and throbbing between her legs alarming her. Fuck, fuck, fuck. Why couldn't she be immune?

"Ethan has those ridges along the sides of his abs too," Ally told Sabrina.

"Logan just has the abs," Sabrina replied.

Marcus dropped his tank top back in place and turned to the guys. "Ever feel like a piece of meat?"

"In all the right ways," Ethan said. "C'mere, baby."

Ally practically flew to him.

Logan crooked his finger and Sabrina floated over to him, smiling.

"Bedroom furniture next," Logan announced, his arm around Sabrina. "Then the boxes and that's everything. I've got a cooler of beer and we'll order some pizza as a thank-you for all your help. Sound good?"

"Yeah, let's finish up," Ethan said, giving Ally one last squeeze.

The men headed to the bedroom.

Ally walked into the kitchen. "Come on, ladies, let's finish packing the boxes. Ethan brought a dolly, so it won't take long to haul the boxes out. Then we're done!"

Sabrina joined them in the kitchen and gave Lexi a sympathetic look. "You okay?"

Lexi threw her hands up. "Whatever! Men, right? Can't live with 'em, can't fuck without them."

Ally giggled and Sabrina elbowed her, shaking her head.

"Back to work," Lexi said, determined to ignore the temptation that was Marcus Shepard.

Even if temptation lived right down the hall.

4

Lexi corralled all of her friends into going to ladies' night with half-price drinks at Garner's Sports Bar & Grill on Tuesday. It had been a while since they'd had a girls' night out, and she was so looking forward to spending time with them without their guys.

She parked and walked briskly to the front entrance, stepping into welcoming warmth. She spotted her friends right away, gathered near one side of the long dark cherrywood bar.

Her heart kicked hard. Marcus sat at the bar too. His back was to her, in a collared light blue dress shirt that pulled tight across his broad back. He was talking to Josh Campbell, the bartender and manager of the place. Now that Marcus was in town Sunday through Wednesday, he must be hanging out with his local friends. She hadn't run into him at the apartment building since he'd moved in two days ago. She could admit to a small pang of disappointment. He'd grown on her despite the rumors and her friends' warnings.

She dragged a bar stool over to the very end of the bar next to Hailey and peered down the bar at everyone. "Hey, ladies, how's it going?"

Mad piped up right away with a big smile. She was the youngest Campbell and a total tomboy. Her hair was growing out awkwardly, shaggy and nearly shoulder-length, dark brown on the top half, fire-engine red on the ends. She was letting it go back to her natural brunette for her upcoming wedding in June. "Hailey's mom and my dad are shacking up. She's moving in next weekend."

"Wow," Lexi said, glancing at Hailey to see how she was taking the news.

Hailey was unusually quiet, her long strawberry blond hair half hiding her face as she focused on petting little Rose sitting on her lap. That was when Lexi noticed Hailey's pink fingernail polish was chipped, and three of her nails were short. Was she biting her nails? Holy shit. This was serious. Hailey never left the house unless she was perfectly made-up from head to toe, no detail overlooked. The woman probably slept with lipstick perfectly applied.

Mad was downright cheerful. "They've been dating for five weeks, but it's pretty serious."

That was fast. Maybe when you found someone late in life, you got serious faster. Both of them were old enough to have fully grown children.

"It's too soon," Hailey said morosely. "I told her that."

Sabrina added her professional relationship counselor opinion. "They seem to be deeply in love. Living together is the next step of intimacy."

Mad slapped the bar top. "Marriage is right around the corner!"

The women launched into much speculation over the possibility of a marriage between the two and how cute it was to see people their age so mushy with love. Hailey remained withdrawn.

Lexi's chest tightened in sympathy for Hailey. "You okay about your mom and Joe?" she whispered.

"Of course," Hailey said, tossing her hair over her shoulder. "I could use a drink, though. Josh is being so slow today." She settled Rose back in her pink doggie purse before gesturing to Josh, probably because Josh didn't like seeing her dog loose at the bar.

Was Hailey unhappy because a possible marriage between

her mom and Joe meant Hailey would be connected to her arch-nemesis Josh forever?

Josh ambled over to them. He'd gotten a haircut, his dark brown hair short on the sides, longer on top, still sexily rumpled. He wore a red flannel shirt with worn jeans. His stubble was approaching beard territory and looked good on him.

"Hey, ladies, what can I get you?" he asked.

"I'll have some pinot grigio," Lexi said. "Thanks."

"Cranberry juice with vodka," Hailey said firmly. "Light on the juice."

Josh gave her a sympathetic look. "Bad day?"

Hailey pasted on her beauty-queen smile. It popped up in high-stress situations. "I'm fine." Rose's head popped up from Hailey's doggie purse; she belatedly noticed Josh and started barking her head off. Her purple striped bow bounced comically in time.

Josh bared his teeth at Rose, took a few more orders from their nearby friends, and went to get the drinks.

Hailey murmured to Rose, taking her out of her purse and cuddling her close. Rose craned her neck around to growl at Josh low in her throat.

A few minutes later, Josh served up their drinks and growled back at Rose. "Hailey, if you can't get your dog to be quiet, take her outside."

Hailey stared at Josh. "You called me by my name. Not princess." Rose quieted, ears perked for trouble as she stared at Josh too. Princess was Josh's go-to sarcastic nickname for Hailey, probably because of her beauty-pageant wins. She had many tiaras to her name. Hailey called him cad, beast, or scoundrel in return. Very entertaining.

Josh smirked. "It's hard to call someone who French-kisses their dog princess."

Hailey gasped. "I do *not* French-kiss my dog!" Rose added her two indignant cents with ferocious barks. It was hard to say who was barkier. Truth was, they'd all witnessed Hailey letting Rose give her sloppy dog kisses right on the mouth.

Lexi didn't judge. There was nothing wrong with loving your pet.

Josh pointed at Rose. "Quiet or you're out."

Hailey scowled and exclaimed over the noise of Rose's barks, "It's ladies' night! We have a right to be here."

Josh rolled his eyes. "She's a dog. Not a lady."

"A girl dog," Hailey said.

"That makes her a bitch," Lexi quipped. "High paw, Rose." She lifted Rose's paw and gave her a little high five, which distracted her for a moment, quieting her down.

"She's also a therapy dog," Hailey informed Josh. She dug around in her purse and pulled out a tiny blue doggie T-shirt. "Here's her official therapy-dog shirt."

"Isn't she supposed to be wearing that?" Josh asked.

Hailey stared at the shirt in obvious distaste and tossed it back in her bag. "It's not a good look for her."

Lexi stifled a laugh and caught Marcus looking over at them and smiling. He stood and headed her way. *Gulp.* She really hoped he'd forgotten she'd said he was an orgasm-inducing eye-fuck the other day. *La-la-la. Super-casual neighbors. Zero eye-fucking here.*

"Just keep her off the tables," Josh snapped at Hailey. He put both palms on the bar and leaned close to Hailey, setting Rose off on another barking rampage. "And keep her away from the bar!"

Marcus stood next to Hailey and held out his palms. "Can I see her?"

Hailey handed Rose over to him, and Rose quieted. Marcus lifted Rose, cooing at her, "Aren't you a beautiful girl?" He held her against his chest and rubbed behind her ear. Rose's little tail wagged like mad.

Marcus turned to Josh. "Try to use some of that rusty charm on the ladies. It works on all species."

Lexi found herself smiling, watching as Marcus shifted Rose, holding her cradled in one arm, belly up. He rubbed her belly with one big hand, and Rose's back leg kicked happily. She really hadn't expected dog cuddles from a hulking male like Marcus, practically oozing testosterone.

Marcus grinned at Josh. "See where a little charm can get ya?" He lifted Rose up to his ear. "What's that?" he asked as though she'd said something instead of just licking his ear. "Uh-huh. This is serious." He turned to Hailey. "Rose says the bows you make her wear are undignified. The other dogs are making fun of her."

Lexi laughed.

Hailey adjusted Rose's striped bow, which had flopped down. "She loves looking pretty. We spend hours grooming. It's her favorite thing."

Marcus shook his head sadly. "She says that's your favorite thing."

"Oh, you!" Hailey said. "Give me her." Marcus handed Rose back, and Hailey clipped a leash to her collar. "Excuse us. We need a quick break outside." Hailey would never say pee. Much too classy.

Mad swooped in, offering to take Rose for a walk. Hailey handed her over without a word. Mad had been the one to take care of Rose before they all gave her to Hailey as a gift. Rose had been part of an intervention designed to calm Hailey the frick down when she was in hyper mode after ending her long-term friends-with-benefits arrangement just as Josh got a girlfriend. Every one of their friends believed Josh and Hailey belonged together, if only they'd stop fighting long enough. Josh was single now, so it was a possibility, however small.

Hailey took a small sip of her cran-vodka before tossing back half the glass.

Josh stared at Hailey, his brows drawing together. "I can't get over how much alike you and your mom look. It's like twins almost." Josh was an identical twin, so he would know.

Hailey pursed her lips. "Yeah, well…"

Josh went on, gesturing to Hailey. "I mean, the hair, the face, even the designer dresses."

Hailey sniffed. "It's embarrassing."

"Why?" Josh asked. "You got good genes."

Lexi turned to Hailey, thinking the compliment might draw a smile, but no.

Hailey took another swig of her drink. "Because she's still trying to look like she's in her twenties when she's not. She dyes her hair to match mine. Hers is actually blond and white, not strawberry blond."

Josh tilted his head. "Do you shop at the same store?"

Hailey scoffed. "You know nothing about women's fashion."

"I know you both look like you stepped out of a glossy magazine at all times," Josh returned. This was true.

Hailey's eyes flashed, her color high. "It's completely different!"

Josh shifted closer. "How?"

Hailey raised a finger. "For one thing she does it because she works at a high-end boutique and *has* to wear their clothes. Besides, she gets a huge employee discount." She finished her drink and gestured for Josh to give her another one.

He didn't move. "Uh-huh."

Hailey gestured again, lifting her glass in the air and shaking it.

Josh ignored her request.

Hailey lifted the glass to her lips, tapping the bottom for the last drop. She set the glass down with a thunk. "And her stuff is this season."

"You mean winter?" Josh asked.

Hailey turned to Lexi. "Order a cran-vodka." She jerked a thumb toward Josh. "The bartender likes to give me a hard time."

"You got it," Lexi said. "Josh, I'd like a cran-vodka, please."

Josh ignored Lexi, his focus on Hailey. "So your mom wears winter clothes?"

Hailey let out a huge exasperated breath. "No. Her clothes are current, on trend, just hit the runways."

He arched a brow. "And yours aren't?"

"No."

"Why not?"

"Because I can't afford it, okay?" Hailey exclaimed. "I

have to project a professional image at all times. Half my work is at the office, the other half networking in the community. How do you think I continually bring in new business?"

Josh remained unflappable despite Hailey's outburst. "If you can't afford designer stuff, then why're you always wearing it?"

Hailey stood and pulled her gorgeous royal blue A-line dress away from her body. "This is two seasons ago! I got it from the consignment shop."

"It's beautiful," Lexi put in. "Why don't you have a seat and relax?" She guided Hailey back to her seat, whispering in her ear, "And keep your voice down." It certainly wasn't going to help Hailey's networking if she spilled all her secrets to the locals. Some of the people around here were real gossips.

"I need another drink," Hailey announced.

Lexi handed over her wine.

"Thank you, Lexi," Hailey replied sweetly. "Only you understand me."

Josh went right back to his line of questioning. "Why don't you just shop at your mom's store with her discount?"

"Give it a rest, Josh," Marcus put in.

Josh ignored him, his gaze glued to Hailey.

Hailey tossed her hair. "Because I'm an independent businesswoman not a clone of my mother."

"Huh," Josh said.

"What's that supposed to mean?" Hailey demanded.

Josh lifted one shoulder. "I thought you came from a snobby elite beauty-queen line."

Hailey's jaw dropped. "You know what? You're the snob!" She jabbed a finger at him. "You judged me from the first moment we met, and you've been making my life hell ever since!"

Josh's brows drew together in apparent confusion. "No I didn't."

"Yes you did!" Hailey hollered at the top of her lungs.

All of their friends exchanged a look of alarm. Hailey was losing it.

"There was a lot of fighting," Lexi put in, rubbing Hailey's back.

Marcus went for a distraction. "Hey, Josh, how about a round of drinks on me?"

Josh stared at Hailey. "I thought we were just messing around."

Hailey got quiet, staring at the bar.

Sabrina leaned close, speaking in a soothing voice. "Maybe there were some hurt feelings that came out as anger."

"Did I..." Josh bent to try to see Hailey's face. "Hailey, did I hurt your feelings?"

Hailey didn't respond.

Josh swore. He leaned down, probably trying to get Hailey to meet his eyes. "I'm sorry. I admit to being pissed off with some of the stuff you pulled, but mostly I found you entertaining. You know, I push your buttons, you push mine."

Hailey raised her head, her eyes shiny with tears, still saying nothing. Josh looked equally distraught.

Hailey never got this upset. This whole thing with her mom and his dad getting serious must've really gotten to her. Everyone looked at Hailey sympathetically and then turned to Josh expectantly. He had to fix this.

Josh offered his hand. "Let's have a truce. A real truce."

Hailey eyed his hand suspiciously.

"We'll go back to the beginning and...fix it."

"It's a good idea," Lexi said. "Shake his hand." Their friends chimed in encouragingly.

Hailey met Josh's eyes. "You'll give me my money back?" That was where their frenemy war had begun. Josh had kept the money Hailey gave him for being her paid escort at weddings. After their falling out, Hailey had demanded it back. Josh always said she had to go back to his place and get it, which Hailey refused to do.

Josh nodded once. "Yup."

Hailey seemed to be considering this. Mad returned with Rose. Hailey gathered Rose close, stroking her behind the ear. "What do you think, Rose? Should I trust the cad?"

Josh looked to the ceiling, but refrained from commenting.

Hailey turned to Mad. "Will you please watch Rose? I'm heading to Josh's place. I'll be back shortly."

Mad's brown eyes were wide as she took Rose. "You're actually going to his place?"

Hailey nodded, her expression grim.

"One minute," Josh said. He hustled back to the kitchen and returned with a guy, who took his place behind the bar. Then Josh walked over to stand by Hailey's side, offering his arm in a gentlemanly gesture that she ignored. Rose began her warning growl and Mad quickly backed away to quiet Rose down.

Hailey looked up at Josh. "I will now restore your rep for my part of the truce."

"No—" Josh started.

Hailey then announced in a voice that could be heard for miles, or at least to all of the local women who'd shown up for ladies' night. "Attention, everyone! I'm going to Josh's den of sin. He's completely cured of any and all problems, and I can't wait." Her tone and expression were closer to a woman going to her execution than about to go to a gorgeous man's place. Hailey lifted her chin, the picture of bravery in the face of her impending doom. "We've declared a truce and are now on good friendly terms."

The bar fell silent, everyone staring at them curiously.

Josh gave her a wry look. "You done?"

Hailey nodded enthusiastically. "Yes, I think that worked."

Josh shook his head. "It's not a den of sin and I'm not the devil. I live in a humble one-bedroom apartment."

Hailey smiled a little, her first real smile of the night. Lexi exchanged a relieved look with her friends. "I always pictured you in a brothel."

Josh laughed. "I always pictured you in a mansion." He offered his hand. "Friends?"

Everyone held their breath.

Hailey slowly extended her hand and shook his hand in one firm up-and-down motion before quickly dropping it.

Josh inclined his head toward the door. "It's a short drive. Come on."

They all turned to watch them go. Josh walked ahead to hold open the door. Hailey walked with her head held high, looking very much like the beauty queen she used to be.

As soon as the door shut behind them, Lexi spoke into the silence. "Holy shit!"

"Pigs must be flying in hell today!" Mad crowed, which made everyone laugh.

Everyone started speculating on how long this truce between Hailey and Josh would last. Of course everyone hoped for the best, but their history was pretty rocky. They really did push each other's buttons.

A half hour later, the door opened and they all turned to find Josh walking in alone.

"Where's Hailey?" Lexi asked.

"She walked home," Josh said, slinking behind the bar.

Lexi immediately texted Hailey to find out that she was indeed home. *Are you okay?*

The group text went mad with a flurry of texts asking what happened.

Hailey replied simply, *I'm home and I'm fine. Goodnight.*

Mad marched up to the bar and got in Josh's face. "Nice going! She's so upset she forgot her dog!"

"I tried—"

"Try harder!" Mad barked. Rose barked too.

Josh shoved a hand in his hair and stalked to the other side of the bar.

Mad left with Rose to return her to Hailey. The rest of them huddled close, debating if they should go to Hailey's place or give her some space. She hadn't seemed like herself tonight, but maybe she just needed some peace and quiet. The question on all of their minds—

What the hell had happened at Josh's place?

Josh refused to comment, so Sabrina called Hailey to get the scoop. She got off the phone only a moment later saying, "Hailey's going to bed early."

It was pretty bad if Hailey wouldn't even confide in

Sabrina. Maybe when Mad showed up with Rose, she could get the details out of Hailey. For now they were all pissed at Josh for upsetting Hailey worse. He was supposed to be fixing things.

Lexi turned to Marcus, who'd been quietly watching the whole exchange. "I feel bad for her. She's really a loving generous person." She lowered her voice. "I actually thought she might work things out with Josh."

Marcus shook his head. "There's plenty of single guys at my bar if she wants to meet someone away from you-know-who." He inclined his head toward Josh furiously scrubbing the bar top with a rag at the other end of the bar.

"I'll mention it to her later," Lexi said. It was long past time for their meddling but well-meaning matchmaker to find her very own happy ending. "How's your mom?"

He took a pull on his beer, taking his time answering. Finally he set the bottle down. "The same. No improvement."

"Did you mention the therapy-dog idea?"

His shoulders drooped as he stared at the bar. "She says a dog is too much responsibility."

Her heart ached for him. She could practically feel the weight of his burden.

He stood abruptly, tossing some bills on the bar. "I'm heading out." He raised a palm to her friends. "Night, ladies." He turned and called over to Josh still furiously scrubbing the bar. "Later, Josh."

Josh tossed the rag under the bar, jerked his chin at Marcus, and then just stood there, jaw clenched, staring off in the distance.

Marcus turned to her, his dark eyes pained, his jaw tight. "Bye."

"Bye," she said quietly, watching him go. For one crazy moment she considered going after him and hugging him or something.

Once she got home from ladies' night, she stopped by Sabrina's old apartment and rang the bell, wanting to check in on Marcus. It had to be hard to be the only one your ailing mom could depend on. She planned to share more about her aunt's agoraphobia and see if there was something that would work for his mom.

He wasn't home.

Maybe he'd gone to check on his mom. No way could she show up there. His mom would have her head on a platter.

She headed back to her apartment, unlocked the door, and sighed. Ladies' night had been a bust with everyone worried about Hailey. It almost made her wish for a time when Hailey would've been cheerfully all over her about finding the One, as if such a person existed. How effed up was that?

5

_____

Lexi had just returned from a trip to the grocery store the next day with the bare minimum to get by for the week—her dwindling bank account never far from her mind—when she ran into Marcus coming out of his apartment down the hall. He was dressed casually in a black hoodie and athletic pants.

He closed the distance between them. "Hey, Lexi, how're you doing?"

She bobbed her head. "Good. How're you?"

"Getting by. How's Lexi's Events? Get any new clients?"

She swallowed hard. She'd really been trying to keep positive about her new freelance career, but it was tough when she hadn't brought in any new business. It had only been a week, but still, tell that to her bills. "Not yet. Working on it."

"It's not easy to start a new business. I've been there."

Her throat tightened, eyes hot at the sympathetic understanding in his voice. "Thanks."

"Listen, I'm on my way back to the city and I'll be at work by four. Why don't you stop by my bar and we'll work out the details for the Mardi Gras event?"

"Really?" Her voice cracked. "But I upset your mom. I told you, you're under no obligation to keep to our original deal."

He flashed a smile that gave her a jolt. "Show me what

you got, Lexi. Maybe I'll hire you for more events and spread the word. My bar is filled with big Wall Street spenders."

She stilled, trying to think it through, the logistics, the timing. Mardi Gras was only two and a half weeks away, which meant it would be tough to pull something good together. On the other hand, she currently had zero clients. "I'll be there, thank you."

"Excellent. Chin up, my friend, you'll get there."

He swaggered away and she watched him go, a lump in her throat. She shook her head at herself. It wasn't like her to be so emotional. She headed into her apartment and set the two grocery bags on the counter. Marcus had given her hope, a lifeline when she really needed one, even after she'd screwed things up with his mom. You know what? She was going to fix this thing with his mom just like she'd wanted to in the first place. She'd go to her house and apologize. And if Lia wouldn't let her in, then she'd slip a note under the door. Maybe she'd even be able to help Lia too, eventually.

She quickly put the food away, grabbed her purse, and headed out the door.

~

Marcus spotted Lexi the moment she stepped into The Burrow later that day in a white knitted hat with a big pom-pom. Not because he was watching the door for her, he reassured himself. Anyone would've noticed that hat. She wore a black down vest over a white turtleneck with black skinny jeans and high-heeled black boots. Winter gear that still showed off her sexy trim body. No big puffy coat for her.

"Lexi!" he called, raising a hand in greeting from where he stood behind the bar.

"Hey." She lifted a hand and gave him a friendly smile.

His chest warmed at the sight, knowing he had something to do with that smile. He was her first client. She crossed to the bar, standing across from him, her brown eyes bright. A gray laptop bag on her shoulder told him she'd come prepared. She took off her hat and smoothed down her hair.

He caught her eye, his lips curving into the half-smile that never failed with women.

Her lips parted, her gaze on his mouth. *Never. Failed.*

"Can I get you a drink?" he asked.

"I'll take some water, thanks."

He filled two glasses. "Why don't we sit in one of the booths?" Three people sat at the bar already, and he figured they could have a little privacy in a booth.

"Sure." She looked around. "This place looks so much bigger than the last time I was here. I mean, I guess it was Saturday night last time."

"Yeah, it can really get packed in here." The Burrow had the look and feel of an Irish pub. It was long and narrow, the dark glossy bar on the right, a few high-top tables in the center of the space, and farther back, there were booths. Upstairs was a private room that could be reserved for large groups, with a fully stocked bar, poker tables, and a pool table. That was where he liked to bring his friends when they ventured out to the city. He lived only a few blocks away.

He made a quick phone call to get a sub behind the bar. Once Sam stepped in, Marcus headed for the first booth, where Lexi was already seated, facing the door.

He sat across from her and slid her glass across the table. "What's up?"

She opened her laptop and booted it up. "I had lunch with your mom today."

He shot up straight in his seat. "What? How? Where? Did she leave the house?"

Lexi met his eyes. "I felt terrible about upsetting her, so I stopped by and apologized. I told her sometimes I stick my foot in my mouth and I was very sorry for stepping over the line."

"And she let you in the house?" he asked, unable to keep the shock from his voice. His mom had said Lexi wasn't welcome in her home.

She laughed. "Why is that so hard to believe?"

He moved right on past that touchy question, figuring it would only hurt her feelings if she knew what his mom had said. "So you had lunch there or you went out? Details, woman!"

Lexi inclined her head. "After I apologized, I told her I'd recently gotten laid off and asked if she'd like to have lunch to commiserate with me. My treat."

He blinked, shocked at the balls on her. To go back there with a humble apology and then offer to buy his mom lunch was above and beyond the call of duty. Lexi had been roped into going there in the first place, and they weren't even in a relationship. Even if they were, he never would've asked her to face his mom alone. He would've run interference for her.

Lexi went on. "She said she loved Ernie's Diner, so I brought lunch from there and we ate it in her kitchen." That was the diner he and his mom used to go to before she refused to leave the house.

His chest ached, his throat suddenly tight with emotion. "But they don't do takeout."

"I worked around that. I sat and had a bowl of soup. Then I ordered her favorite chicken pot pie, got one for myself, and told the waiter to wrap it up."

"Clever," he murmured. *And why hadn't he thought of that?*

"I'm a problem solver," she said in a singsong voice.

She was something. He suddenly wanted to hug her, but she was across the table from him, and he couldn't figure out a way to do it without being awkward.

"We talked about you." She smiled mischievously, her eyes practically dancing with glee. "I told her how little Rose loved you, and guess who she told me about?"

He rubbed his forehead, avoiding eye contact. "Who?"

"Bitty Kitty!" She flexed her nonexistent bicep muscles and attempted to do a gruff he-man voice. "Big hulking teenaged Marcus hiding a tiny white kitten in his jacket pocket." She laughed. "She told me all about how you tried to smuggle her home, covering up her meows with fake coughs and sneezes."

He jabbed a finger at her and said in mock anger, "Hey! Bitty Kitty was a special cat. Not like the regular kind. She'd come when I called her like a dog."

She didn't laugh this time. Instead she looked at him warmly, tenderly, like she actually *liked* him at his embarrassing worst. "Your mom felt bad you couldn't keep her because of the apartment rules. She told me you visited Bitty Kitty at Ben's grandmother's house for years."

He grunted. "It was nice of Mrs. Walsh to take her in."

"You loved her."

He jerked his chin. The love of his life. "She lived to be sixteen. Lost her a couple of years back."

"Aww, Marcus! You should get another cat."

He shook his head. "Nobody can replace Bitty."

She smiled at him, another warm tender smile. He swallowed hard, surprised at how much that warm tender smile affected him, feeling kinda warm himself, even in the throes of mom-induced embarrassment.

"Anyway," she said, "I gave your mom the number of a local psychiatrist that Sabrina recommended. The woman specializes in agoraphobia and does phone sessions to help her clients learn to handle their anxiety and reenter the world."

Something in him cracked open, a flood of emotions hitting him all at once—pure elation, gooey affection, tremendous relief. He was grateful too, so humbly grateful he couldn't even speak, his eyes stinging.

Lexi must've noticed because she looked down at her laptop screen, giving him a moment to pull it together. "It went okay. She took the suggestion in the friendly well-meaning way that I offered it. I'll text you the doctor's info so you can arrange payment if she does call."

He found his voice. "Lexi." He waited for her to meet his eyes. "Thank you." He put a hand over his aching chest. "From the bottom of my heart."

She shrugged, her eyes shifting away. "No big."

"No. It's very big. Thank you."

She met his eyes, her voice quiet. "You're welcome."

"Does she still think you're my girlfriend or…"

"I acted like you were *all that*—" she waved a hand airily

"—you know, just to encourage her to keep talking to me, so I think she assumed we were together."

He couldn't get past the fact that his mom was cool with Lexi now. Not only that, she didn't seem to mind them being together. He would've heard about it right away if she still objected.

He couldn't help his smile. "I'm all that, huh?"

She rolled her eyes. "Don't let it go to your head. I was making amends, fixing what I screwed up for you since you were nice enough to give me this job when I really needed one. Should we get started?"

"Is it okay if we let her think we're together a while more? I think it's helping her. I know that sounds weird, but—"

"Marcus, it's fine. Really. Besides, I'm getting all the goods on you. She even showed me your baby pictures. Classic naked-butt pose too." She grinned.

He shook his head, smiling. "What can you do? Proud mom."

"And you were hung!"

He barked out a laugh. "Shut up, you pervert."

She laughed. "So I've got tons of ideas for your Mardi Gras event. But first, what kind of budget are we talking here?"

"Whatever you need." He'd pay anything to help out Lexi, who'd already made more progress with his mom in one lunch than he'd managed in the last two months.

Her eyes widened. "You don't have to worry about money?" she asked in a hushed voice.

He took a sip of water. "It's like this. Jake Campbell lent me the money for this bar. I paid him back within a year and then I invested in Dat Cloud. Before it went public." Dat Cloud was Jake's company and had made Jake a billionaire. Marcus had made out very well too.

"Before it went public," she echoed. He could see her putting the pieces together. "You hit the mother lode!"

"Shh. I'm doing well. Now I can invest for fun, so I'll invest in you for fun."

She stared at him, clearly in shock. Obviously she didn't

know him very well. He'd do anything for his friends, and Lexi now qualified as friend *numero uno.*

He made a big show of rolling his eyes and heaved a sigh. "Do I have to do everything? Hurricane drinks, beads, and purple, green, and gold decorations."

She snapped to attention. "How about a speed-dating masquerade?" She made a pretend mask with her fingers around her eyes. "Just an eye mask, so you can still see most of the person's face. And if you give the ladies half-price Mardi Gras cocktails, you could really pack them in here."

He rubbed his stubbled jaw. "Keep talking."

"We incorporate social media into it too. Royalty is a big part of Mardi Gras, so we make a king and queen of the bar contest. The first twenty people who enter will make a poll on social media to get votes."

"Liking that social media idea."

She went on enthusiastically. "We can have people make floats, like miniature floats out of small cardboard boxes, and then vote on the best one."

He grimaced. "That sounds messy."

"We could set up a couple of long tables away from the bar for people to make them." She pointed over to the space. "Speed-dating rounds back here in the booths, royalty contest at the bar. Then staff can rotate people through stations. There's something for everyone."

"I like most of that, except the half-price cocktails. I think they'll pay full price for this event."

"Okay, then we can make cool cocktails too. Hurricanes, but also purple, green, and gold drinks." She turned her laptop, clicking over to some saved cocktail recipes. "Anything look good?"

"Whatever you pick is fine."

She smiled. "You might be my easiest client yet." She looked around. "I don't think you'll have room for a live band with everything else, but we can make a cool jazz playlist, some nice mood lighting, like twinkly white lights. Some traditional New Orleans food."

"We usually do jambalaya and gumbo."

"Excellent. Maybe add some Cajun shrimp and grits. Ooh, maybe we could get some alligator meat too."

He made a face. "You ever eat that?"

"No, but it sounds very New Orleans, doesn't it?"

"You ever been to New Orleans?"

"No, but I read."

He smirked. "I've been there. It's amazing and the women flash you for beads." He took a drink of water, hiding his smile.

"I always hated that. We should give out beads to the guys with the biggest dick."

He spewed his water.

She cracked up.

He grabbed a bunch of napkins from the table dispenser and wiped his mouth. "You're gonna get the cops in here on indecency charges."

She lifted one shoulder. "Same thing. Tits, dicks."

He stared at her. "It is not the same thing at all."

"Tomato, tamato. Anyway, we could give out a bead necklace when they walk in and then for prizes for different games. Trivia, best float, funniest float, cutest speed-dating couple, stuff like that. The person who has the most necklaces at the end of the night wins something. Maybe a fifty-buck bar tab so they'll return and bring their friends."

"That sounds good to me. I'll probably need you to help run it."

"Absolutely. I—" She stopped and stared at someone over his shoulder.

He turned to where his longtime waitress, Ellie, stood in her favored tight ripped jeans and skin-tight thermal shirt that emphasized her large breasts. That combined with long wavy brown hair and striking blue eyes meant she raked in the tips with the male customers. She was also his best employee—here with him from the beginning—and she managed the bar in his absence. "Hey, Ellie. How's it going?"

Ellie smiled. "Hey, boss." She turned to Lexi. "Hi."

"Hello," Lexi said.

Ellie turned back to him. "How long are you going to do this living-in-the-burbs thing? We miss you around here."

"Not sure," Marcus said, thinking of his mom. He forced a smile. "No worries with you around. You keep it running smoothly." He was lucky he could count on her to step in while he was living part-time near his mom. He patted his jeans pocket, suddenly remembering the key he'd left in his office. He'd get the checkbook while he was there too for Lexi. "Excuse me a minute, ladies, I'll be right back."

He stood and turned to go.

Ellie pointed toward the kitchen. "I left you something sweet in the fridge."

"You're killing me." He slapped a hand over his flat stomach. "You know I'm off sugar." He kept walking.

Ellie called out to him, "That's cuz you're already sweet, sugar."

He laughed and kept going.

~

Lexi went back to her laptop.

"What're you two planning over here?" Ellie asked.

Lexi lifted her head, surprised Ellie was still there. "He hired me to plan a Mardi Gras event on Fat Tuesday."

Ellie smiled. "Sounds fun. I'm usually in the know, but it's been tough with Marcus out in the burbs half the week."

"I'm sure he'll fill you in."

Ellie leaned down, speaking in a conspiratorial tone. "I hope you don't take Marcus's flirting too seriously. I mean, most women do."

"No worries."

Ellie glanced over her shoulder before whispering, "There was a woman who took him way too seriously. She was one of many he was dating. When he dumped her, she tried to kill herself."

Lexi's hand went to her throat. Did Marcus know the devastation he'd wrought? A woman tried to kill herself over him? That was serious. She swallowed hard. "How do you know this?"

"Her brother Nate is a regular. He tells anyone who'll listen to steer clear of Marcus."

"Was this recent? Does Marcus know?" She couldn't imagine Marcus not caring if he did know.

Ellie glanced over to where Marcus was now striding toward them, and turned back, leaning close to Lexi to confide, "The only reason he screws around so much is because of his divorce. That bitch really did a number on him."

Lexi hadn't known Marcus was married before. How well did she know him, really? She didn't want to believe the bad rumors about him. She liked him, and he'd been good to her. But maybe that was how he was with all women, which was why they ended up devastated.

Ellie put her hands on her hips and called out to Marcus in a saucy tone, "Whatcha got there, boss man?"

Marcus held up a keychain. "Apartment key." He handed it over.

"Thank you," Ellie chirped. She stuck the key in her jeans pocket and walked away.

So Ellie had an open invitation to the boss's apartment.

Lexi clenched her teeth, taken aback by the stab of jealousy. Dammit. Marcus had gotten under her skin. She found herself wanting to believe in him, wanting to believe he'd changed, that he was no longer a cheating, lying player with a long trail of shattered hearts.

An uncomfortable lump of emotion lodged in her throat. She swallowed it down, reminding herself it was better if she and Marcus were just friends.

6

———

Marcus took his seat in the booth and smiled at Lexi. She did not smile back. "Got the checkbook. I'll pay you half up front."

"Thanks," she said tersely.

"Something wrong?"

"You and Ellie together?" Her tone was flat.

"No."

"She has your apartment key."

He studied her for a moment. The fact was Ellie was renting the apartment next door to The Burrow. He'd recently bought the adjoining building, which would soon have a coffee shop on the lower level. He gave her low rent by Manhattan standards and a pay bump since she'd stepped in as part-time manager in his absence.

"Are you jealous?" He kinda hoped she was because that meant she was into him. She had said he was an orgasm-inducing eye-fuck of a man with his shit together and she couldn't think of anything better than that. She'd definitely grown on him too.

She stared at her laptop. "It's none of my business."

"That's true." Was this a good time to make a move? Or would it screw everything up? She was making such great progress with his mom he didn't want to do anything to jeopardize it. "Lexi, I don't play where I work."

She typed furiously, not looking at him. He waved his fingers in front of her face, and she finally looked up from the laptop. "What?"

He leaned close, lowering his voice. "I know you got the goods on me from my mom, but there's more to me than a handful of buff baby pictures." He thought that might coax a smile from her, but she wasn't budging. "All I'm saying is maybe you don't know me as well as you think you do."

She gave him a sour look. "I know you're a flirt down to your bones. Some women might take it to heart. Not me. Other women."

"Flirting is just my way of being nice."

She shut her laptop with a snap. "So if you flirt with women to be nice, how're you nice to guys, then?"

He wasn't sure why she was asking, but whatever. "I play basketball with them, buy them a beer. Bro stuff."

"Do that with me."

"You want me to treat you like a guy?"

She nodded emphatically. "I'd like that very much."

"All right. Well, I guess we could play pool. I'd do that with my bro. There's a table upstairs." *In a very private room.*

"I have to get back. Live by the train schedule." She tucked the laptop back in the bag and then just sat there, staring at him for a solemn moment.

He waited, unsure where she was at. He'd never felt so off-balance with a woman before. One minute he was sure she was into him, the next she was fleeing the scene. Maybe she was nuts. But would a crazy woman be such a generous friend, helping him out with his mom's condition? No. It must be something about him that sent her on the run. He decided right then and there to treat her exactly like she'd asked to be treated. Like a guy. That was the only way to keep her comfortable, to keep her from running away from him.

He smirked. "When I kick your ass at pool, you can buy me a beer."

"Ha! You'll be the one buying me a beer." She grabbed her

down vest and purse, shifted like she was going to stand, and then seemed to change her mind, staying in place. "Can I ask you something?"

"Anything."

"I've watched you flirt with every single one of my friends, but you never flirted with me. Why?"

"I thought you'd bite my head off," he replied honestly.

She frowned, her brows drawing together. "Am I that scary?"

"Not scary. More like a back-off attitude around men."

Her lips pressed together. "It's complicated. I like men for some things."

"Not going to touch that one."

She went on, her voice earnest. "I just haven't been too impressed with men as a species. Overall."

"Well, on behalf of my species I say *thrbt!*" He blew a raspberry.

She shoved her arm in her down vest. "Mature."

"You realize we're the same species with some complementary parts?"

She got her vest on and threw one final look at him that he could not interpret. Irritated? Intrigued? He'd never had so much trouble reading a woman. "You sound smart," she said. "Much smarter than when you flirt."

So I sound like an idiot when I flirt? Thanks a lot!

He narrowed his eyes. "This is how I talk to guys. You're now a guy to me." Yup, he was really going to win her over now. He couldn't help getting defensive when she threw jabs like that. Sure, he might look like a hulking mass of muscle, but underneath all that, he had feelings, sometimes very sensitive feelings. He'd sooner parade around naked in Times Square than admit any of that shit.

She cocked her head. "So you normally talk down to girls. Hey, darling, hey, sweetheart, aren't you a pretty little thing?"

He clenched his jaw. "No, I charm them. That means a lot of compliments. Don't need big words for those, do I?"

"What did you do before you owned this bar?"

"Why?"

"Because I'm trying to understand what makes you the way you are."

The way you are? That sounded bad. "How am I?"

She gestured for him to hurry up. "Just tell me what you did before you owned a bar."

He shrugged one shoulder. "After I graduated from Penn—"

"Penn!"

"Yeah," he said slowly. "Penn. Economics degree. I headed to Wall Street, dollar signs in my eyes. Got sick of that frantic life, moved to a hedge fund; then I..." He stopped himself. She didn't need to know that.

"What? Tell me."

"It's stupid. *Really* stupid."

"If you went to Penn, you can't be stupid. It's written all over their Ivy walls." She leaned close, her voice lowering. "Come on, tell me."

He grimaced. "I got married."

She straightened abruptly. "Why was that stupid?"

He ran a hand through his hair. "Because a man in love does stupid things. Moved to Vegas for a year—that's where we met, I know, I'm a walking cliché—and I got some crap job at a casino. Blew most of my savings spoiling her. Long story short—it ended. Moved back home and started all over again."

"Why did it end?" she whispered. Like whispering would make it easier for him to say.

"That's not something I talk about with the guys."

She batted her eyes. "Can I be a girl just for this talk?"

He gave her his sexy half-smile. "Sure, darlin'. None of your sweet-ass business."

She laughed and offered him a fist bump, so he gave her one. "See ya."

"Hold up. The check." He quickly wrote out the amount, folded it in half, and gave it to her.

She peeked at the check and looked up at him. "Marcus, this is very generous."

He tapped the table. "And I expect a kick-ass event in return."

She beamed a smile at him. "Thank you so much! You won't be disappointed." She left the booth and strode toward the door.

He turned to watch her go, striding with purpose, and found himself smiling. He was in the friend zone, but somehow it didn't matter. Because he was no longer numb with a woman like he'd been since his divorce four years ago. He felt everything—her jabs, her warmth, her delight. There was only one explanation—

He adored her.

Marcus drove to Ethan's place back in Eastman late Sunday morning, looking forward to working out with Ethan's weights. He'd just come from his mom's house. The bad news was she hadn't called the psychiatrist; the good news was she was no longer against him seeing Lexi. Not that he would've let that stop him after getting to know Lexi better. He'd been numb for so long with the women he'd dated. Flirt and charm, dinner and wine, bed and gone. It had gotten old, but he hadn't changed what he did. Why was that? Too busy or… maybe he just didn't know any other way to be.

Ethan's fiancée, Ally, was working her part-time gig this morning, so it'd be bro time. It still baffled him how Ethan had gotten himself engaged—given he was a tough hard-ass—when Marcus had gone out of his way to be a charmer. And all Marcus had gotten for his efforts were a few laughs and a lot of emptiness.

Geez. Was it so much to ask? Why couldn't he find someone like Ethan had? Why couldn't Lexi be that someone? He deserved that much, didn't he?

Maybe he didn't. Maybe that was why it had never happened.

What the hell did Ethan have that Marcus didn't have? They

had similar fucked-up backgrounds, similar upbringings with the Campbell family, similar practical outlooks. Growing up, Ethan had been tough with no respect for authority. It was their honorary dad, Joe Campbell's influence that had set Ethan on his career path as a cop. Good thing too. Punk-ass with a chip on his shoulder wasn't much of a career. But with Ally, Ethan was different—smiling, laughing, lit up with pure joy. How did Ethan get from point A to point B? Marcus felt stupid asking. Everyone knew he never had a problem getting a woman. But lately he'd realized it wasn't just any woman. It was the *right* woman.

By the time he got to Ethan's townhouse, he was so agitated that Ethan took one look at him and immediately steered him toward the treadmill. His friend's dining room was a home gym. Pretty sweet setup with a treadmill, barbells, smaller dumbbells, and a rowing machine.

"Get a hard run in," Ethan said. "It'll make you feel better." Ethan's short dirty blond hair was already damp with sweat, so he must've gotten a head start.

Marcus went to the treadmill, and Ethan took a seat at the rowing machine, quickly getting into a steady rhythm.

He started the treadmill slow for a warm-up run, glancing over at his friend. Ethan was only a year older than him, his expression dialed to hard, authoritative, and *don't fuck with me*. Not surprising given his training as a cop. Marcus amped up his run, working hard, trying to get out of his head. Ethan silently rowed across the room, completely focused on his form.

By the time Marcus finished a hard run, his heart rate was up, tension was down. He slowed the treadmill for a cooling off period. Screw it. He was here, Ethan was here, it wouldn't hurt to ask for a hint about getting a woman to adore him. But if Ethan laughed at him, there'd be a smackdown. It could get ugly. Ethan was not someone anyone messed with, especially now that he was trained to subdue criminals. Marcus didn't care. He couldn't take being laughed at for such a serious problem.

Summoning all the casualness of asking about the weather, Marcus posed the question that might unlock all of his future happiness. "Hey, Eth, how'd you get Ally?"

Ethan glanced at him and went back to rowing. "What do you mean how did I *get* Ally? You don't get a person."

"I mean, uh, how did you hook her? She looks at you like you're…I don't know, like she adores you. She lights up, you know?"

Ethan stopped rowing and grinned, his whole face lighting up with that love-happiness he wore like a second softer skin. "I love the way she lights up. You asking for Lexi? I saw the way you look at her."

Admit nothing. He didn't need that kind of pressure, the guys watching him go for it and possibly fail. "I don't know. Just in general."

Ethan smiled some more. "I've only ever loved Ally. But I guess what I did could work for you. First we did the friend thing. I invited her to do stuff I like. You know, to see if we were compatible."

Marcus turned off the treadmill. "Stuff *you* like?" That went counter to all of his experiences with women. He went out of his way to do what they liked. Had he gotten it wrong all these years?

"Yeah. I invited her hiking with my hiking club, real low-key, no-pressure situation. Did that a few times." He frowned. "She hasn't been hiking with me for months though. She has a fifty-degree rule. Has to be fifty degrees or higher." He lifted a hand, showing a certain level. "I even got her these thin thermals and kick-ass hiking boots. It's all about the right clothes to enjoy the outdoors, ya know? But she's like, no go, her face is cold, but she won't wear the face mask because it feels weird." His forehead crinkled for a moment like he was still trying to figure out a solution to the hiking problem. "Anyway, as soon as it warms up, we'll get back to it."

This was the longest conversation he'd ever had with Ethan. The longest sentences his friend had ever uttered too. "What else did you do?" Marcus asked.

Ethan went back to rowing. The man was a machine. "I took her fishing."

Marcus puzzled over that. Ethan loved fishing, but

Marcus didn't know a lot of women who did. Ethan was a real outdoors enthusiast. "What else?"

Ethan rowed merrily along. "I took her to a cookout. She loved the s'mores." He turned to Marcus, smiling so big his blue eyes crinkled at the corners. "You were there. Remember the party by the lake?" Ally and her friends had organized that party.

"So you basically made zero effort?" Marcus had put in tons of effort with women, making reservations at all the best restaurants in the city, pulling strings when he had to for a primo table. Not only that, he bent over backwards to find the right compliments, and didn't he make sure the woman got off first every single time? How was that fair? Ethan had done zip.

Ethan stopped rowing and scowled. "I made an effort. Geez. Aren't you listening? I took her to all of my favorite things. That's how she got to know me."

"And then she's madly in love with you? Eth, I've seen the way she looks at you. It's like you can do no wrong." He put his hand up to the ceiling. "Like you're up here."

Ethan smiled, stood and stretched. "Yeah, well, she's like that for me. We're sure of each other. We both really appreciate what we have."

He still couldn't believe making zero effort had gotten Ethan to where he was now. "So how did it get to that level?"

Ethan shrugged. "When I knew she was into me, I made my move. You'll know when the time's right."

"Yeah, I guess." Except he was more confused than ever. He'd made plenty of moves before, and none of them had gotten him a woman who loved him and only him. "So then, one day you were just in love."

Ethan shifted closer. "It's like, I thought about her all the time, I got psyched to see her, I got to a point where it was hard *not* to be with her. Plus I had all this stuff going on with Peggy's death." That was his foster mother. "It made me more open to love. You have to be open to it. But once you are, you feel everything."

Marcus blew out a breath and turned off the treadmill. "Deep."

Ethan nodded.

Marcus headed over to the dumbbells. "What do you do now that it's too cold for hiking and fishing?"

"Hang around here." Ethan looked away, mumbling, "Other stuff."

Marcus pounced. "What kind of stuff? Could you possibly be doing things she likes?"

Ethan dropped to the floor in a plank position, holding his body perfectly still. "It's not like there's a game on every night."

"You watching girly shows?" Marcus teased.

Ethan held his plank, his voice defensive. "I'm just keeping her company. Some of those house shows teach you stuff. We're saving for a house, you know. And she's been helping out Hailey on the weekends with the wedding planning and sologamy stuff, so ya know, there's shows that can be helpful for that too. There's like a show for everything." He switched to rapid push-ups.

Marcus grabbed a pair of dumbbells and did some slow arm curls. "Uh-huh. Wait, sologamy?"

Ethan grunted, finished his reps, and then stood, explaining how women marry themselves in a sologamy ceremony and commit to their own happiness. "It's all about empowerment. Ally and all of her friends did the sologamy ceremony together. Now Ally offers it as an add-on to weddings for a bonding thing for the brides, bridesmaids, and any other woman who wants to join in. It's legit."

Marcus was speechless. To hear Ethan speak with such authority on women's empowerment was a shock. He was just such a *guy* guy. He'd definitely changed since being with Ally. It wasn't good or bad, really, just different.

Ethan picked up a barbell and lifted it over his head. "And we still go out. Like, you know, the mall and shit."

He was getting the girly picture. "You go shopping with her?"

"Shut up." He lowered the barbell to the floor. "You asked

me for advice, I gave you advice."

"All right, touchy. I'm happy for you, man. Really."

Ethan heaved the barbell overhead again. "I don't care what we do—shopping, fishing, whatever. I love her, and her happiness means everything. I would watch every home show, every bridal show, every sappy romantic movie." He lowered the barbell to the floor and met Marcus's eyes with a serious expression. "I would hold her purse and watch her try on clothes until the cows come home. I would run out in the night to buy her favorite ice cream or tampons—"

"Whoa! TMI."

Ethan smiled goofily. The weirdo. "It's like that."

Marcus watched Ethan working out for a few minutes, thinking on that. He just couldn't see it. Tough Ethan in the feminine hygiene section? At the register paying with witnesses and everything? Finally he told Ethan, "Fuck, man, that's some twisted shit."

Ethan smirked. "That's love. When you're open to that serious-as-fuck level, it'll happen for you."

Marcus gestured to let him have a turn with the barbell and they switched places. "That is terrifying."

Ethan picked up the dumbbells. "It's not for the faint of heart. Takes a big man to take a fall like that. It humbles you, makes you realize what really matters. She's my heart." His voice choked.

Marcus's throat tightened at the emotion in his formerly stoic friend's voice. "Cool. I'm glad you got that."

They finished their workout and headed to the kitchen to rehydrate. Ethan poured a couple of glasses of water and sat with him at the small kitchen table.

Ethan gave him his assessing cop look. "What's the deal with Lexi?"

Marcus took a long drink of water. "I don't know. We're friends, I guess." And she wanted him to treat her like a guy, which put him in this weird place of wanting more and not knowing how to get it. He couldn't imagine actually following Ethan's advice—inviting Lexi to do his favorite thing, working out. Buying her tampons? *Shudder.*

Ethan slapped the table, and Marcus startled. "Life's freaking short. If you think you got something, go for it. Ask her to do what you like. Maybe not lifting weights, that's not so easy for a woman. What else you like?"

"Basketball."

"You want to play basketball with her?"

"I have season Knicks tickets."

Ethan tilted his head, considering. "Yeah, I guess that could work. If she wasn't too bored. See, hiking or fishing, there's always something to do. That's what I like about nature."

"Uh-huh." Marcus was an indoor cat.

Ethan took a drink, set his glass down, and lifted a palm. "I just remembered something else. Zach says from an anthropological point of view, the dominant male is highly valued for a mate as a protector and provider for the young. Not dominant like pressing the woman down. More like showing you have the strength to fight off enemies, protect the family, and bring home the gift of food. You should talk to Zach. He's got a real deep understanding of courtship and marriage customs."

Marcus blinked. Ethan was getting surprisingly academic. Ethan had grown up in the same foster home as Zach, who was now a professor of anthropology. Zach was always spouting some kind of animal-instinct stuff. Not very helpful in modern times.

"So I should bring her some meat or fish?" Marcus asked as a joke.

"That could help," Ethan said enthusiastically. "And make sure you get in good with her family and friends. It's biological. Zach explained it. Approval of the mate and all that." That part actually made sense. And Zach was about to get married in May, so maybe there was something to all this anthropological stuff.

His head was swimming with information, and he wasn't sure how much was actually relevant to his current situation.

Fuck it. He'd try it all.

7

Lexi wasn't as immune to Marcus as she'd like to be. She'd told herself it was best if they were just friends, but she found herself thinking about him way too much. First of all, he was smart. That was even sexier than his body, which was plenty sexy already. Second, he had some tender sweetness hiding under all those bulky muscles. Like the way he generously offered her a job and took care of his mom and cuddled little Rose and…oh, just everything. Now that she'd glimpsed the sweetness, she couldn't unsee it. Smart, sexy, sweet—the S trifecta guaranteed to make any woman a soft, swooning, sighing *mess*.

How could this be the same man who left women devastated? There had to be some kind of reasonable explanation for the terrible rumors about him. Maybe his ex-wife had screwed him up so badly he'd spiraled out of control for a while but was better now. He seemed stable. Or maybe she was in denial. It wouldn't be the first time. And hadn't that bit her in the ass with her cheating ex?

She sighed, opened the refrigerator, and stared in the vain hope that dinner would magically produce itself. Bummer. The kitchen fairies failed her again. She shut the door and grabbed the box of Kix cereal from the cabinet. She popped a few crunchy Kix in her mouth, chewing thoughtfully as she poured a bowl. Maybe she was just making excuses for Marcus because of the unexpected S trifecta.

She poured some milk into the bowl, grabbed a spoon, and headed for the sofa. It was Sunday night and she figured she'd flip channels, see what was on. She'd just settled onto the sofa when the doorbell rang. Now that her friends had moved out, nobody ever stopped by unannounced. Oh, shit. Was it Marcus? He was probably back in town by now. She looked down at her ratty old purple sweatshirt and gray sweatpants, had a brief moment of panic, and then said screw it. She didn't need to look good for him. They were just friends. If it was him. Why was she suddenly hoping it was?

The bell rang again.

"Coming!" She hurried over and peeked through the peephole. Her heart pounded, all of her suddenly flushed with heat. She opened the door to Marcus standing there in a black leather jacket, jeans, and black work boots, looking like her bad-boy wet dream.

"Hey," she said casually. "Wasn't expecting you."

He held up a brown bag that smelled wonderful. "Brought wings. Knicks are away tonight. Mind if I watch the game on your TV, bro?" She *had* told him to treat her like a guy. This was a nice safe friends thing. And wings instead of Kix sounded pretty darn good.

She gestured widely. "Come on in."

He smiled, his dark eyes lighting up. "Excellent." He followed her in. "I haven't gotten a TV yet for my temporary place. Mostly I watch stuff on my laptop. The game's better on a big screen."

"Have a seat," she said, heading to the kitchen. "I'll get plates and a roll of paper towels. Wings can get messy." Her stomach growled in anticipation. "You want something to drink?"

"You got any beer?"

"No. I've got milk or water."

"Water, please."

By the time she got everything over to the coffee table, Marcus had already made himself at home, man-spreading across her green sofa. His legs splayed wide, his arm stretched along the back of the sofa, his gaze on the game. Bro time. He'd been considerate enough not to start eating. The take-out boxes on the table were untouched.

She opened one. It even had celery with ranch dressing.

"That one's medium hot," he said. "The other one's spicier. I wasn't sure how much fire you could take."

Her head whipped toward him. Something about his tone held some subtle innuendo. Two could play at this game. "I can take it all."

His dark eyes gleamed. "Wild, hot, or blazing?"

"Yes." Her voice sounded breathy.

He smiled his sexy half-smile. "Good to know. I'll remember that for next time." He winked, piled some wings on a plate, and went back to the game.

She sat next to him and pretended like everything was totally normal. Just two bros hanging out watching the game. Except she knew she was playing with fire. She piled some wings on her plate and took a bite. Mmm…so good.

"This is so much better than what I was going to have for dinner," she told him.

He glanced over at her. "Yeah? What's that?"

"Kix cereal." She waited for him to act judgmental. Clearly he was into health and fitness.

"I always keep Life cereal around for when I'm too tired to cook."

"Oh." She smiled a little. "I thought you only had protein shakes and lots of red meat."

"Usually I eat pretty healthy, but Life's not too bad for you. Pretty low sugar."

She relaxed and ate some wings. "So who's winning?"

"Knicks. But it's just the first quarter." He drank some water. "Want me to explain the game?"

"I know it. I'm just not a big fan of it."

He set his glass down. "And I just barge in asking to use your TV. Go ahead and put on what you like."

"It's okay. I have an older brother. Sports was on all the

time at home growing up." She picked up a wing. "Anyway, you brought me a hot meal."

They ate in silence except for the sound of the TV and Marcus's occasional whoop when the Knicks scored. It was kinda nice to have company again. Now that her friends weren't just down the hall, she spent a lot more time at home alone. Probably didn't help that she was working from home. So far she'd set up shop using Hailey's suggested lawyer, made business cards, and networked as much as possible both online and in real life, but she should probably get up to speed on the financial side of owning her own business so she'd be prepared. She glanced at Marcus. He might be able to help with that with his economics degree and the fact that he owned his own business.

She waited until they were both done eating *and* for the commercial to ask him. She knew better than to try to talk to a male sports fan in the middle of the game.

"Sure, I could walk you through the financial side," he said.

"Thanks, I really appreciate it." She gathered up their trash and dumped it inside the take-out bag. "Figured I should be prepared right from the start. It's kind of nerve-racking being your own boss. I mean, everything is on me."

"Being your own boss is awesome. Sure, there's a learning curve, but you'll get it."

"Thanks." She took the trash to the kitchen, a little more optimistic about her future career.

She returned to the living room, and he flashed a smile that made her heart kick up a rapid beat. He looked happy to see her, happy to be with her, and damn if she wasn't just as happy about the situation. This was not good. *Boundaries.*

She flopped on the sofa and propped her feet on the coffee table. He did the same, his arms spreading along the back of the sofa, one of them right over her head. She straightened and shoved at his arm. "You can't man-spread across my entire sofa. Respect the personal space."

"Sorry. Didn't realize I was man-spreading." He put his arms at his sides. "I was just relaxing."

She stared at the game, irritation building in her. She didn't want to want him, but here he was looking all bad-boy sexy, bringing her a delicious dinner, being all accommodating. His musky sexy scent mixed with hot sauce was driving her insane with lust. That was *it*. She had to know the truth about him, so she did what no woman in her right mind would do to the sexy bad boy in her apartment, call him on his shit.

She grabbed the remote and hit pause on the game. "I heard you don't believe in monogamy." That was her polite reference to his cheating. "So why did you get married, then?"

He stared at her, his expression somewhere between surprised and annoyed. Probably because she'd interrupted the game.

"Well?" she asked.

His expression closed, his voice tight. "I believed in monogamy all the way up until my marriage fell apart."

"So then you cheated?"

He frowned. "I never cheated. She cheated on me with multiple men."

Her stomach rolled, realization sinking in. He'd been hurt just like her. She could only imagine how hurt he must've been by someone he'd loved enough to marry. That must be why he didn't believe in monogamy. "I'm sorry. That sucks."

"Yeah, it did, and I'm over it. That was four years ago. Can you put the game back on?"

She wasn't quite done. "That's why you became a cheater, dating three women at the same time. It was because of your ex-wife."

He snatched the remote from her hand, but he didn't press play immediately. Instead he glared at her. "I said I'm not a cheater. After my divorce, I was in a tailspin. I wasn't ready to be exclusive with anyone, and I told that to every woman I dated. Everything was aboveboard. They could see whoever they wanted while I did the same. And that was also a while ago. I haven't been with anyone in months."

She worked hard to hide her surprise. A virile sexy man

like Marcus hadn't been with anyone in months? She suddenly wanted to hug him. She was so relieved to hear there were completely reasonable explanations for his behavior. Still, she'd feel better if she just put it all out there, really get to the bottom of his bad reputation and find out he was the good guy she wanted him to be all along. "Why haven't you been with anyone?"

He spoke through his teeth. "Because."

Not much of an answer. "Why would you ever need to see three women at the same time?"

He clenched his jaw. "Because it was fun."

"And then it stopped being fun?"

A muscle ticked in his jaw. "Yes."

She puzzled over his obvious irritation. Was she not supposed to ask completely relevant questions? "What about Ellie?"

"What about her?"

"You gave her the key to your apartment."

"Not where I live. My rental. Now can we watch the game?"

She wanted to soothe him, but she didn't know how. All she knew was that he had a tender side that must've been deeply hurt for him to act the way he did. And if he really was over his ex now, maybe that meant he was going back to his normal way of being. Problem was, she didn't know him well enough to know what was really him and what was Marcus in a tailspin.

She scooted closer, nudging his arm with her shoulder in a soothing gesture. "I was just curious because…you're here and you smell good and you brought me food."

He set the remote down and gazed at her steadily. "I believe in monogamy again. I want that. I've seen all my friends find their partners, women they adore, and…I'm tired of feeling empty. Tired of playing games. Just so damn tired of the whole scene."

Her adrenaline spiked, heart-racing, pulse-pounding excitement rushing through her at this new side of Marcus. "You want a woman to adore?"

He leaned close and smoothed her hair back behind her ear. "Actually, I already have a woman I adore." He gazed into her eyes, warm and tender and sweet. And she melted. Just melted.

"Me?" she asked just to be sure.

He smiled. "Yes, you." He wrapped his arms around her and hugged her. Not what she'd been expecting. She rested her cheek on his chest, his heart pounding under her ear. Was he scared like she was?

She looked up at him. "My ex cheated on me too. I found them in our bed. It was his place, so after we broke up, I lost my home too and our shared dog." Her voice choked. She *loved* that dog. They'd gotten Tig, a boxer, together, but she was the one who trained him and took care of him.

"Lex, that sucks. So sorry that happened to you."

She swallowed over the lump in her throat. "I haven't been with anyone since then, many, many months. I haven't even been tempted."

He gazed into her eyes, and she thought he might say something flirty about temptation, but he surprised her. "We'll get your dog back."

She sat up, her heart squeezing tight. "Thanks, really, that means..." Her voice cracked, and she coughed to cover it. "That means a lot, but my ex, he, uh, took a restraining order out against me. I could be arrested."

"Back it up. Tell me the whole story."

She told him the Tig story. After she'd caught Noah cheating on her, he'd kicked her out of his townhouse and kept Tig. Not one to give up on the love of her life, she'd tried to steal Tig back early the next morning. Noah had caught her struggling to get the big dog into the backseat of her Subaru. Tig hadn't been cooperating, probably thinking he was going to the vet. Next thing you knew, Noah had the dog and she had a restraining order against her.

"And that was my short-lived life of crime," she finished.

Marcus pressed his lips together, clearly taking her loss seriously. "If you give me the address, I'll steal him back for you. He doesn't have a restraining order against me."

Her lips parted, breathless, her heart swelling with pure affection. "You'd do that for me? Breaking and entering, stealing?"

"Hell yeah. I get that love for your pet."

Her lower lip wobbled and she bit it, her eyes stinging. "That is the nicest thing anyone has ever offered to do for me." She wiped at the wetness leaking out of her eyes. "But the truth is, I don't have a yard for Tig, and Noah moved back to his parents' house. He lost his job. They have a huge fenced-in yard and a girl dog, a little Yorkie, that's like his bestie. He seems pretty happy."

He stared at her. "And you know all this because?"

"Well, I had to check on Tig."

"So you stalked your ex?"

"No! I emailed him and he wrote back and sent me a picture of Tig with Sugar."

He cupped her face with his big hand. "Aww, Lex. You've got a little sweet hiding in there, don't you?"

"Shut up."

"You shut up." And then he kissed her.

And he was good at it.

Damn.

His lips moved over hers, smooth heat, his tongue tracing the seam of her mouth, seeking entrance. She opened for him and the kiss turned wild, all lips and tongue and teeth. She scrambled into his lap, wrapping her arms around his neck, pressing herself against his hard muscular body, losing herself in his taste, his scent, his glorious mouth.

His hands were under her sweatshirt, skimming up her bare back, bringing electric heat wherever he touched. She ground against him, the hard bulge in his jeans hitting just the right spot, drenching her with desire.

He broke the kiss suddenly, breathing hard. "I should go."

She grabbed his head. "Are you kidding me?"

But he wasn't kidding. He peeled her hands off him, set her off his lap, and stood. She reached for him, but he stepped away. "Lex, I want to take it slow with you."

"I'm cool with it."

He blew out a breath, looking at a point over her shoulder. "I don't do that rush-to-bed thing anymore. You've got to get me to at least a third date nowadays."

She gaped at him, standing in front of her and not touching her. Ooh, wasn't this the ultimate irony? She'd found the best turn-on—a reformed bad boy—which was also the worst tease. At least she hoped he was reformed. She still had some niggling doubts, mostly due to what Ellie had told her, but could she really trust Ellie's word? It sounded like work gossip.

He leaned down and dropped a kiss on top of her head. "See you soon for a second date."

"This was a date?" *In her ratty sweats?*

"Yup." Then he walked out the door.

She stared at the door, still in shock. Did that seriously just happen? What guy walked out in the middle of a hot makeout session with an eager lusty woman? What guy walked out on his favorite team's game? She turned to the TV. It was still paused at the beginning of the third quarter and they were tied. That was not at all a sure win. He should've wanted to know who won, should've stuck around to find out.

It was because of her. Because he adored her. A warm tingling feeling seeped through her, giving her a hot shiver. This was a more dangerous situation than she'd realized. Lethal.

He was trying to *romance* her.

And despite all of her defenses and natural resistance to any and all vulnerability, her heart squeezed with the possibility of her very own true romance. Was it really possible the man she'd thought was everything she despised was actually everything she'd ever wanted?

8

Marcus was hunkered down at Garner's Sports Bar & Grill, watching the end of the Knicks game. The fact that he had to haul himself across town to avoid the temptation of Lexi down the hall was a conundrum. He'd made his move—pure instinct—but then he'd had to stop because this woman was different. He didn't want to do the same old wine-dine-bed, though he wouldn't exactly call chicken wings and the Knicks a wine and dine. He'd intended it to be a friendly thing like Ethan had suggested, getting to know each other by doing what he liked. He'd even incorporated Zach's advice to bring meat.

He let out a manly sigh. Now that they'd crossed the line —he'd admitted he adored her—the pressure was on to do something special, but what? He supposed he could ask her what she liked to do, but what if he got stuck doing embarrassing girly things like getting his nails done or antique shopping or, the absolute worst, shoe shopping.

"Yes," he whooped as the Knicks won. He'd missed a tense third quarter, but the fourth had been awesome as the Knicks kicked ass.

Josh moved over to him, working the bar as usual. "Want another beer?"

He considered Josh for a moment. His dark brown stubble

was nearing serious beard territory, like it had been at least a week since he'd shaved. Was Josh going through something? Maybe the fallout with Hailey last week at ladies' night had hit him hard. Or maybe he was missing his ex. They'd been together for two months, probably Josh's longest relationship. But that was back in December, more than two months ago. It had to be Hailey.

Marcus waved the offer of a beer away. "No, thanks. You okay?"

"Sure, fine. Why do you ask?"

"Hailey."

Josh set his jaw, close-mouthed like always when Hailey's name came up.

Marcus had grown up with Josh like a brother, which was why he didn't pull any punches. "What the hell happened that night? She was so upset she walked home in the cold of a February night *and* she forgot her dog. You know how she loves her dog."

Josh clenched his jaw. "I offered her a ride back."

"What'd you do?"

He threw his hands up. "I didn't do anything!"

Marcus cocked his head. "What'd she do?"

"None of your damned business."

Interesting. "Okay, okay." Though it was odd that Hailey was to blame if she was the one who walked home in the cold. Something wasn't adding up.

Josh shifted away, checking on the other customers, mostly guys there to watch the game. Marcus waited for him to refill beers before gesturing him over.

Josh took his time getting to him. "What?"

"I need some date ideas besides dinner."

Josh relaxed. "Who you asking out?"

"Lexi Judson."

Josh grinned. "Got the full name going on, huh? Sounds serious. Well, what does she like to do?"

"I don't know."

"You can ask her, you know."

And be forced to endure girly stuff? "Just give me some ideas."

Josh looked to the ceiling. "Let's see, besides dinner, you could do lots of cheap stuff like a hike and picnic, walk along the boardwalk and try to win a prize for her on one of those games, take a walking tour of Clover Park and let her window-shop, buy her ice cream, stuff like that."

"It's February, though. Kinda cold for most of those ideas."

Josh rattled off more ideas. "Ice skating, bookstore with a café, bar with a dance floor." He gestured at him. "You've got The Burrow. Take her there for a drink and, if she's cool with it, take her up to the private room to play pool, dance, *whatever*." He winked. "That's three activities at once and it costs you nothing."

Marcus laughed. "I wasn't trying to be economical. I was just trying to make it special."

Josh glanced up and down the bar, probably checking on the drink situation. He turned back to Marcus. "You have to actually know her well to do something special."

"What'd you do on your dates with Clarissa?" That was his ex.

Josh tsked. "If I tell you, I'll have to kill you before you blab to the guys."

"That bad, huh?"

Josh blew out a breath and gave him a rueful look. "Let's just say way too much yoga and green drinks were involved."

"Guess we know why that one didn't work out."

Josh grabbed a rag and started cleaning the bar top.

He thought about The Burrow idea. "The thing about the private room is it's just so private."

Josh tossed the rag under the bar. "You don't want to be alone with her? *You?* That's rich."

"She's different."

Josh rolled his eyes. "Oh, geez, here comes the sappy stuff. Just invite her friends, make it a party."

"A party date."

Josh lifted both hands. "Why the hell not?"

"All right. I'll check if the private room's available." He texted Ellie, who was on tonight. A few minutes later she got back to him. The room was booked Friday and Saturday nights. Thursday was available, and he told her to reserve it. He lifted his head. "So what's the easiest way to get in touch with everyone?"

"Just tell Hailey what you have in mind and she'll do the rest."

"You got her number?"

"Yeah. She won't care that I gave it to you. She lives for this shit." Josh pulled out his phone, tapped it a few times, and then wrote the number on a napkin.

Marcus grinned. "Not gonna let me see your phone, huh? You guys in a mad texting war? Or is it sexting?"

Josh shoved his phone in his jeans pocket. "Don't be ridiculous."

Someone was ridiculous and it wasn't Marcus. He kept that to himself because Josh, like always, had come through.

"Thanks, man."

Josh grunted.

Marcus texted Hailey, who responded right away, *I'm on it! Sounds fun!* Then he texted Lexi to invite her.

Lexi: *Are you going to run away after the party?*

His neck burned. *I didn't run tonight. You're special. That means we take it slow.*

Majorly inconvenient I got a reformed bad boy yanking my chain. Get ready for an ass kicking in pool.

He barked out a laugh. He'd definitely made the right move. A special date, taking it slow. No girly stuff, either, and Lexi was on board.

See you then, he texted.

You live down the hall. I'm sure I'll see you before then.

How about lunch with my mom tomorrow?

Sure. Are we always going to do stuff with other people?

He smiled some more and texted back. *For now.*

Guess my vibrator will get a workout.

He chuckled. *I would like to see that.*

Come on over.

Not yet, darling.

Don't you darling me!

Not yet, horny woman.

Truthfact.

He smiled and caught Josh's knowing look. "She's funny," he told him.

"And…" Josh drawled, "he joins the ranks of the undead."

"Undead?"

Josh nodded sagely. "Ever notice how the guys resemble zombies once they're hooked? Yes, dear, whatever you want. I like what you like, honey." His lip curled. "Pathetic."

Marcus couldn't stop smiling, thrilled to be included with the love zombies. He was smart enough not to mention Josh had done the whole yoga and green drink thing for his woman. Instead he pointed at Josh. "And then there was one."

"Yeah, yeah," Josh said. "Last man standing. The only guy with his head on straight."

"For now."

Josh gave him a light slap on the cheek. "Idiot."

Lexi floated through her week, all thanks to Marcus. He was just so much better than the kind of guys she was used to dating. He spent zero time bragging about how great he was and never even made a move on her. It was like he just wanted to spend time with her. On Monday after their lunch at his mom's house, he'd bought her a coffee at Something's Brewing Café back in town, and they'd just talked and talked. He told her about growing up with the Campbells, about some of the crazy shit that had gone down on Wall Street, and about how much he loved owning The Burrow. She told him all about her previous job and the ideas she had for going beyond event planning to party planning for busy professionals. On Tuesday they shared takeout for lunch at her place, talking over her business plan. And now today, Wednesday, he was taking her out to lunch before he had to drive back to the city for work, where he'd stay through the rest of the week. He was only living part-time in Clover Park. She'd see him at The Burrow tomorrow night too for his party.

She checked her look in the full-length mirror in her bedroom. Marcus had told her to dress nice for the restaurant, so she'd paired her white blouse with a plum-colored pencil skirt, black stockings, and high-heeled black ankle boots. She'd left her hair down, light on the makeup. Nerves skittered through her. Today felt more like a date, going out someplace nice for lunch.

The doorbell rang and her heart leapt. *Calm down.* She headed for the door, took a deep breath, and answered it.

Marcus flashed a smile and held a bouquet of red roses out to her. "For you," he said warmly.

She sucked in air. Not just because he was breathtakingly gorgeous when he smiled, it was just all his warmth and romantic intentions focused on her made her almost woozy. He really was beautiful—his dark hair styled back smoothly, chiseled cheekbones, square clean-shaven jaw. His large muscular body filled out a white button-down shirt, the sleeves rolled up to the elbows, and gray pants that must've been tailored to his exact measurements.

"Thank you," she said, clutching the bouquet to her chest. She stared at the roses, admiring their lush petals just beginning to bloom.

Marcus cleared his throat. "So you want to put them in water or take them with you?"

Her head jerked up. How long had she been standing here admiring her roses?

She laughed. "I'll put them in water. Just a minute." She went inside and he followed.

"Hope you like Italian," he said.

"I love it."

"Great."

She pulled a vase from a high cabinet, filled it halfway, and arranged the roses. Then she set it on the coffee table so she'd see them as soon as she returned. She crossed to him and he gave her a warm smile.

"You look beautiful," he said, offering his arm.

She took his arm, feeling weak in the knees. She'd never known that was a real thing before today. "Thank you. You're beautiful too. I mean, man beautiful." She shook her head. "Handsome."

He laughed and led her out of the apartment. "So how do you feel about sharing dessert? Some people want it all to themselves. This place has the best tiramisu, second only to Venice."

"I can share. You've been to Venice? I've always wanted to go."

"I've been to a lot of places. I like to go somewhere different on every vacation."

They drove to the wealthy town of Greenport for lunch, Marcus telling her all about his awesome travels around the world—plenty of countries in Europe, but also Peru, Costa Rica, an island off the coast of Africa, Japan, and Australia. He loved to scuba dive whenever he could. He was so easy to talk to, she completely relaxed.

He parked, walked around to her side, and opened her door for her. Then he tucked her hand in the crook of his arm for their walk to the restaurant. He made her feel special, like he was really into her. In her experience, guys played it cool, games and all that shit. Not Marcus.

"Is it scary to scuba dive?" she asked. "I'd worry about running out of oxygen."

"Nah, it's great, you'd love it. I got certified before Australia so I could explore the Great Barrier Reef. The coral was amazing, tropical fish in all shapes and colors. We even explored a sunken ship."

"I've snorkeled before in St. Thomas, but never tried scuba. I've heard it's great in Hawaii."

"Oh, yeah, both scuba and snorkel are fantastic in Hawaii. Things slow down at work for me in August. We should take a trip out there."

She bit her lip. He was inviting her on vacation? The underlying assumption that they'd be together in the future warmed her all over, but made her a little nervous too. What if they planned something and things fell apart? It was only February.

He smiled down at her and winked. "No pressure. I just thought it'd be fun."

She met his dark eyes and took a flying leap into risky relationship territory. "I'd like that."

He smiled widely. "Then it's a date."

She couldn't stop smiling. And she didn't even care that she must look like a complete dope.

They reached the restaurant and Marcus opened the door for her, ushering her inside. He spoke to the maître d' and they were shown to a table in the corner right away. The place was filled with square tables covered in white tablecloths with soft mood lighting in recessed lights and glowing red wall sconces. Several large landscape paintings of Italian vineyards decorated the walls.

The maître d' helped her into her seat. Marcus took the seat across from her.

She put her napkin in her lap and whispered, "This is so nice."

"Wait until you try the food. The steak Florentine is outstanding."

She opened the menu, took a look at the prices, and seriously considered ordering a salad. This was ridiculously expensive.

A few minutes later, the waiter brought over the specials, and Marcus asked for a wine recommendation, checked in with her, and then ordered them a bottle. Merlot from Tuscany. No price discussed.

She leaned across the table to whisper, "Marcus, you're very generous, but you've already offered me an event with a generous budget, and I'm afraid this is too much."

He leaned close. "This is our first official date and I want you to feel special."

"I do, but—"

"That's all that matters." He sat back in his seat. "Please just enjoy. You're the first woman I've spent time with that cut through the numbness I've felt since my divorce. Your delight is mine too, your happiness makes me happy, and even your jabs are fine because I feel everything with you. Do you know how special that is? How special you are?"

She swallowed over the lump in her throat. "I will really try not to jab."

He laughed. "Just be yourself. I like who you are."

"I like you too," she managed.

They smiled at each other like fools.

The waiter arrived with the wine and gave her a small amount to taste. Her eyes widened. "It's wonderful!" The best wine she'd ever tasted.

"Excellent," the waiter said, pouring her a glass.

"Excellent," Marcus echoed, his gaze warm on hers.

She couldn't seem to look away, caught in thrall. He was romantic and gorgeous. His only physical imperfection was the slight bump in his nose. As soon as the waiter left, she asked Marcus, "How'd you break your nose? Boxing?"

"Flag football with the Campbells. It was an accident. Mad fell on me and got me with her hard head."

"Aww, little Mad?" Her friend Mad was six years younger than him and petite.

He pressed his lips together. "Actually it was boxing. The guy was much bigger than me, like a frigging giant."

She laughed. "Uh-huh."

"Really!" He gestured for how tall and wide the guy was.

She shook her head, smiling.

He took a sip of wine, his dark eyes intent on hers. "Tell me more about you. Favorite place, favorite food, favorite wine, very important to know the wine since I own a bar—tell me everything that's important to you."

She stared at him, stunned. No man had ever asked what was important to her.

He waited, looking back at her expectantly.

And because he really did seem to care about her, she rattled off the answers. "Favorite place is Manhattan. I just love the energy, all the people and activity. Favorite food would be a tie between chicken marsala and the ro-jis that my mom makes. They're like a Chinese hamburger, but instead of beef, it's seasoned pork that's been cooked all night in cardamon and cloves, and I don't even know what else is in it. Plus the buns are homemade."

"Your mom's Chinese?"

"She's half Chinese, also part Irish, Italian, and Puerto Rican." She lifted a lock of her stick-straight dark brown hair. "My hair is from the Chinese side."

"Your hair is like silk. I love it."

She felt herself flush. There was a time she was desperate to look like some of her friends with waves or curls, but her hair was uncooperative and, it turned out, those friends wished their hair could be as straight as hers. "Thanks. People are always curious about my ethnicity, mostly because of my hair, tan skin tone, and the downward slant of my eyes."

"Does it bother you?"

"Actually, yeah. It's like they want to pigeonhole me for some reason. Some people are rude. Like they'll say, 'What are you?' Some people just guess." She cocked her head in imitation of the rude people. "Latina? Asian? Mixed race?"

Marcus scowled. "So rude. And what do you say?"

"I tell them I'm an American mutt because it's none of their freaking business."

He grinned. "I knew you'd have a good comeback. Everyone's a bit of something here. I'm a mutt too."

She smiled, and then he unexpectedly barked, startling her. She cracked up. Some people from nearby tables looked over, and she tried to calm herself, but then he started growling and woofing, and she lost it.

Finally when she calmed down, she wiped her eyes and took a sip of wine. "This is the best wine I've ever tasted. This is my new favorite."

"Then I'll be sure to keep it in stock at the bar."

She shook her head. "You're almost too good to be true."

"And to think you didn't like me when we first met."

"I liked you okay."

He wagged his finger at her. "I caught the evil eye you sent my way on more than one occasion."

She bit back a smile. "Caught that, huh?" She lifted her palms. "I just thought you were a man-whore."

He snorted. "I thought you were a man-hater, so I guess we're even." He gestured her closer and she leaned in. "Truth? I always thought you were hot."

She grinned. "I thought you were cute too."

"Cute?" He wrinkled his nose in pure disgust. "You don't reduce this hunk of manhood to cute!"

"Pleasant?"

"Nope."

"Lovely."

He gestured her on. "Getting closer."

"Darling."

His voice dropped to a husky tone. "All right, you can call me darling, sweetheart."

She melted into a puddle of lovey-dovey couple goo.

And she never quite recovered. The meal was delicious, Marcus kept up a steady stream of questions, wanting to get to know her, and he did his part in sharing more about himself. It felt like they were old friends. Except for the occasional smoldering looks he gave her.

By the time he dropped her off at her apartment, she was dying to get him alone. She stopped at her door and turned to him. "You want to come inside?" *And I mean that as dirty as it sounds.*

He placed a palm on the door above her head, and she flushed hot, his musky sexy scent making her crazy. He dipped his head, leaning close, and her pulse skyrocketed. She closed her eyes, nearly vibrating in anticipation.

His lips met her cheek in a chaste kiss.

Her eyes flew open.

He straightened, his voice gravelly. "See you tomorrow, sweetheart." Then he turned and strode away.

She sank against the door. "Bye, darling," she whispered.

She'd never uttered such sweet words in her life, would've found it embarrassing if her friends heard, but just saying them made her feel warm and tingly all over. She could scarcely believe this romance thing was actually happening for her. It was incredible. He was incredible.

She sighed, lost in the wonder of it all. She finally understood what ailed her lovey-dovey friends because now she was infected with it too. All it took was one wonderful man.

Holy crap, she was in love.

It scared the hell out of her. Her trust in men was so low it was really hard not to think the worst of guys. Growing up with a cheating, lying father, then watching her brother repeat the cycle, and then experiencing it for herself with her ex—when she should've *known* better, should've seen the signs—all of it made her want to turn away from Marcus.

She let herself into her apartment and stopped short at the glorious sight of her roses in bloom. The reminder of his romantic gesture made her warm and gooey. She couldn't walk away never knowing what might have been. Her gut instinct told her he was worth the risk.

It was time to take a chance on love.

9

———

Lexi drove to The Burrow with Hailey the next day, their other friends all coupled up and driving with their guys. Hailey was at the wheel in her beloved orange Mini Cooper convertible. She even had a small fake daisy in the cup holder. Rose was curled up asleep in her cozy Sherpa-lined bucket seat in the backseat.

Lexi was ridiculously excited about seeing Marcus again after their fantastic date yesterday. He'd texted her earlier today saying how much he was looking forward to seeing her. Swoon! She was dying for more than a chaste kiss on the cheek tonight. She'd dressed to tempt in a black long-sleeved skin-tight dress that ended mid-thigh with black pumps. It didn't matter what he dressed in because he was always unbelievably sexy. Chemistry would do the rest. Speaking of simmering chemistry…

"How's things going with your mom and Joe?" Lexi asked Hailey. "Do they like living together?"

"I guess," Hailey said flatly. "She says she's in love with him." Normally Hailey would be ecstatic about love. She considered herself a love junkie—it was on her official wedding planner business card—and lived for romance, whether it was in a book, a movie, or real life.

"You're not happy about it? Joe seems great."

"It's not Joe that's the problem." Hailey flicked her long strawberry blond hair over her shoulder and hit the accelerator through a yellow light. They were in the city now, only blocks away from The Burrow. "She falls in love easily. It won't last. I just don't want Joe to get hurt. He already had his wife abandon him with six kids! He hasn't had anyone serious since. Mad is all excited that we might become sisters if they get married, but when my mom flakes, which she always does, Mad won't be so keen on me anymore by association."

"She's your best friend. I'm sure she won't blame you for that."

"It'll leave a really bad impression. Every time anyone in the Campbell family looks at me, they'll see my mom and how she hurt their dad."

"Why do you care so much what the Campbells think of you?" Lexi suspected it was Josh's opinion that mattered the most to Hailey.

Hailey sighed. "It's just that they're the closest thing to a stable family I've ever had. I mean, Mad makes me feel like family, so does Joe, and I guess I don't want to lose that."

They were a pretty cool family, and she could see why Hailey might be worried about them associating her with her mom since they looked so much alike. "Well, I guess it's still early days, right?"

Hailey honked at a taxi that had cut her off. "It's been almost seven weeks. Ask me how I know this."

"She's oversharing with you?"

"Way, *way* oversharing. Apparently Joe is an animal in bed. Dominant, don't ya know? What can you expect from a cop? She likes the handcuffs. Do I *need* to hear this from my mother?" Her voice echoed loudly in the tiny car.

Lexi winced. "I get the feeling you don't get along with your mom."

Hailey sighed. "I'm trying, you don't know how hard I'm trying, but it's like she was always more of a roommate than a mom to me. She didn't want the responsibility of a kid, but she was stuck with me. My dad died when I was three, and he wasn't around much anyway, from what she says. I mean, I know she loves me, but…" She took a deep breath. "She was very flaky when I was growing up, not showing up to work, getting fired a lot. It was scary for me. We were homeless twice because she didn't pay rent and we were evicted. I started on the pageant circuit in my teens, trying to earn money for college so I could make my own more stable life. At least with the pageants, she stopped being flaky. She was so thrilled I was doing them because she thought I was following in her footsteps. The pageants led to her modeling career. Anyway, she started working at that shop we went to for Mad's bridal party stuff, just for the employee discount so she could buy me nice dresses."

"So it sounds like she's been stable for a while, then, right? Maybe she just had some growing up to do."

"Maybe. I guess I just wish she'd been grown up when I really needed her, you know?"

"Parents, right? We'll probably screw up our kids too in some different way."

"Not me." Hailey slapped the steering wheel to emphasize her point. "I'm going to read every parenting book on the market and follow them to the letter."

"Errr, well, I guess that wouldn't hurt to brush up on, but…don't you kinda have to wait and see what your kids are like?"

Hailey lifted her chin. "I will mold them into model citizens."

"Hmm…" *Poor kids.*

Hailey craned her neck, looking all around. "Start looking for a parking space. So how's things with you and Marcus?" Lexi had filled in her friends earlier that they were now a thing.

She beamed, sharing the wonderful news she hadn't dared to say out loud. "He adores me."

"Awwww! That's so sweet! I'm so happy for you. You know I wasn't sure about him at first because he just flirts with everyone and, of course, we all know his rep, but hey! Good on you. So you must not mind the flirting?"

She swallowed hard, her previous happiness fading a little. "He's just being nice." A warning bell went off in her head. This was just like her mother, making excuses for her dad's lecherous behavior. No, Marcus wasn't like that, he was one of the good guys. "He said he believes in monogamy now."

"Yeah?" Hailey chirped. "What changed?"

Lexi tensed. What had changed? How had he explained it again? "I guess just him seeing so many happy couples. He's a good guy. He was just screwed up for a while because of his ex-wife, but he's changed now."

"Oh, I didn't know he was married before. Okay, well, if you're fine with everything, no worries."

Lexi set her teeth. Clearly Hailey disapproved of Marcus. "Josh is flirty with lots of women that come into the bar."

"Josh isn't my boyfriend."

Hailey put her blinker on, pulled to the side, and waited for a parking space behind a car that was leaving. She turned to Lexi. "I'm just looking out for you. One thing I've learned through my years as a wedding planner and love junkie is that the relationships that work out are the kind where the couples don't try to change each other. They love and accept the other person exactly as they are."

"You taking notes?"

"Actually, yes." She glanced at the car slowly pulling away in front of them. "I've got tons of notes on every successful relationship I've been witness to, especially once I started the Happy Endings Book Club." She hit the gas and neatly fit her little car into the vacant space. "I started it as a singles book club and, since no men ever joined, it became my personal mission to see every single one of you happily settled with the man of your dreams. You were the last single lady in there, and now that you have Marcus, my work here is done."

Hailey turned off the car and they both got out. Lexi waited while Hailey snapped on Rose's leash and took her for a potty break. She'd figured the matchmaking in their book club had been Hailey's agenda all along. Now Hailey was the only single woman left in the Happy Endings Book Club.

"What's up with Josh?" Lexi asked. "What happened that night you went to his place to get your money? You've been so close-lipped about it."

Hailey busied herself arranging Rose in her pink doggie purse, which coordinated with her long white wool coat, pink scarf, and high-heeled white boots. Probably dressed to kill under the coat. She started walking at a brisk pace.

"Hailey?" Lexi pressed, keeping up with her.

"Nothing to report on Josh." Hailey stared straight ahead, chin up. "From now on, I'll be applying all the most effective dating techniques to my own life and search for my happy-ever-after in earnest. Maybe I'll meet someone tonight."

Lexi stared at Hailey. Josh wouldn't be here tonight since he was working, but Lexi and her friends had always thought Josh was the obvious choice for Hailey. Their sexual chemistry was palpable. And who cared if they were always fighting? The minute they hit the sheets, the tension would be neutralized and they'd get along great. Although…they were very different. Hailey was ambitious and driven, always dressed up and made up like she was about to be photographed for a glossy magazine. Josh, on the other hand, was laid-back, mellow, and dressed like he'd just grabbed whatever was handy when he rolled out of bed, mostly flannel shirts, T-shirts, and faded jeans. Hmmm…maybe sexual chemistry wasn't everything. Besides, something had gone down that night at Josh's place that seemed to have made a permanent rift between the pair.

Hailey was babbling away about how she was going to conduct a serious Mr. Right search just as soon as she could find the time in her schedule, but all Lexi could think about was Marcus. She couldn't remember ever feeling like this, jittery with excitement, actual butterflies in her stomach over seeing him again.

She and Hailey walked inside The Burrow and spotted their friends in a group near the end of the bar. Not everyone was here. Mad had a big paper due (she was finishing up her last semester of college), and the parents in their group had stayed home, but everyone else had made it. She was especially happy to see her formerly single-in-solidarity friend Missy, back from her romantic getaway with her fiancé, Ben.

"Missy!" She ran over and hugged her. "Look at this tan!" She gestured to her face. Her formerly pale friend glowed. Her dark brown hair was even showing some auburn highlights from the sun, probably her natural red shining through. "How was Aruba?"

"Amazing!" Missy gushed, which said something because Missy was very low-key.

"Did you wear the bikini?" Lexi asked. That had been a gift from Ben. Basically just string.

"Once," Missy said, exchanging a secret sexy look with Ben. He grinned, showing his adorable dimples.

Lexi held up a palm. "Say no more."

Missy laughed. "It was wonderful. Really, really special."

Ben put an arm around Missy's shoulders and gave her a small squeeze.

Lexi looked around for Marcus and found him standing on her left just outside the employees-only door. He was talking to Ellie, who was smiling up at him in a midriff tee and tight jeans. Sure, she had large breasts and a tiny waist—the kind men drooled over—and the striking combination of long dark hair with blue eyes, but that didn't mean Marcus had intentions. Ellie was his employee and they were just talking. Dammit, now she was tense. Hailey had gotten in her head with the flirting stuff. She was extra sensitive to that with her past experiences with men. *Stop it.* This man was worth taking a chance on. She blew out a breath, telling herself to chill.

She lifted a hand and called his name. No response. He was so deep in conversation with Ellie he didn't even notice her.

"Marcus!" she called as she walked toward him. Still didn't notice her.

Be cool.

She closed the distance, standing so close to Marcus she

could feel his body heat. And he *still* didn't notice her! He was thoroughly engrossed in a low hushed conversation with Ellie.

"Hi!" she said brightly. "I'm here."

Marcus's head jerked to her, and then he flashed a devastatingly handsome smile that made her pulse thrum and her body flush with heat. He murmured something to Ellie and finally shifted his attention to her. "I was waiting for you." He leaned down and kissed her cheek. "How're you doing?"

"Fine." *Not jealous. Nope, not me.*

He gazed down at her warmly. "Awesome."

Ellie gave Lexi a tight smile. "I'm having some trouble with a clingy ex. Marcus had to walk me home last night and check the apartment to make sure it's safe." She turned to Marcus. "You're coming up tonight too, right? After the party?"

"Sure, sweetheart," Marcus said in a soothing voice. "I don't want you to worry. Tomorrow I've got the security alarm guy coming in to set you up."

Sweetheart. Suddenly Marcus calling her sweetheart yesterday didn't feel as special. She'd nearly forgotten he said that to all women.

Ellie looked up at him, widening her eyes, playing helpless girl to big strong man. "You know I appreciate that, but it's not the same as letting him know I've got a muscled man like you standing guard."

He laughed. "I want to know you're safe when I'm not here."

Lexi's stomach clenched, their intimate conversation excluding her once again.

"I'll see you later," Marcus told Ellie.

Ellie gave them both a small wave and headed through the employees-only door.

He's just helping her out. He's a good boss.

Marcus took her hand and gave her an appreciative once-over. "You look beautiful. I'm loving this dress."

She relaxed. This was the Marcus she loved—warm, tender, sweet. "Thanks."

Marcus guided her toward their friends. "I'm going to tell everyone to head upstairs to the private party. Ellie will take care of things downstairs."

A few minutes later, they all went through the private door and upstairs, Lexi and Marcus in the lead. She'd been in the upstairs private room once before with her friends for a singles mixer arranged by Hailey. The space was dimly lit, cozy and comfortable, with dark red drapes drawn over two long windows. Dark wooden round tables were scattered around the room, where they'd played poker before. A bar and pool table stood across the room.

Marcus went behind the bar, right away playing bartender. Next thing she knew, music piped through speakers in the high corners of the room. Soft, slow dance music. He called to her. "They're playing our song!"

She laughed, shaking her head. He kept insisting she owed him a dance because she hadn't danced with him at the Valentine's Day dance. She crossed to the bar and took a seat on the end. "I'm guessing they're all our song?"

He gave her his sexy half-smile, his dark eyes locked on hers. "Whatever's playing during our long-awaited dance will automatically become our song."

"I hope it's a good one," she said with a hint of *sexy times ahead*.

"I'm sure it will be," he replied with a wink.

"Uh, should I just help myself to a beer?" a guy asked loudly.

Lexi startled, suddenly aware of Ben standing by her side, the bar lined with her friends watching her and Marcus with open curiosity. She felt herself flush and turned back to Marcus. "Better get back to serving."

"Merlot?" he asked, looking only at her.

"Preferential treatment," Ben grumbled.

She bit back a smile, her heart kicking harder. "Sure."

"You got it." Marcus opened a fresh bottle of merlot, the muscles in his forearms flexing sensually. "It's the Tuscany merlot you loved so much yesterday at lunch."

She gasped. "Marcus! Seriously? How did you get it in stock so quickly?"

He grinned. "I scoured Manhattan for it and found it in a restaurant on the Upper East Side. Bought it earlier today."

She beamed at him. "You're amazing. Thank you."

He smiled back. "No, you're amazing. Thank *you*."

Ben groaned.

"Hey," Marcus said to Ben, "we all put up with your lovesick puppy eyes plenty with Missy."

Missy laughed from Ben's other side.

"You in love, Marcus?" Ben asked in a teasing voice.

Lexi stilled, both wanting to hear Marcus's answer and afraid he'd laugh it off, making her feel stupid for all her sappy love feelings.

Marcus met her eyes for a long moment, and she held her breath. "I do adore her."

The air whooshed out of her lungs, all of her nerve endings alive and electric. A man who owned his feelings in front of the guys? Extraordinary.

Her friends chimed in a collective, "Aww!" The guys chuckled.

Ben muttered, "I'm getting cavities from the sweetness."

Marcus grinned and turned to her friends. "What can I get you ladies?"

"I'll have a beer, thanks," Ben said dryly, walking around the bar and getting one himself.

Lexi sipped her delicious wine while Marcus served each of her friends with a warm smile and liberal use of "sweetheart" and "darling." He was charming as always, her friends eating it up, but she wasn't worried. She and Marcus had something really good going between them.

Finally the group broke up, some playing pool, some of the guys starting a poker game, but Marcus had other ideas. He walked around the bar and offered his hand. "Dance with me."

She took his hand, and he drew her to a corner of the room, away from the noise of the pool table and the poker game.

They could hear the music, thanks to an overhead speaker. He led her in a slow waltz, his heat intoxicating, his large hand resting lightly on the small of her back. The unexpected gentleness of his touch surprised her. She was used to a rougher touch from men, especially since she favored big muscled men, not always aware of their strength. But Marcus was aware. He was careful with her, and that made her feel special.

She caught Hailey's eye at the pool table. Hailey did a little excited wiggle and quiet clapping, which made everyone else at the pool table look over, smiling and talking quietly to each other, probably talking about her and Marcus dancing alone in the corner.

"Maybe we should go back to the party," she told Marcus. "Everyone's staring at us."

"Nope. You're not weaseling out of this. I get at least one dance." He leaned down to her ear, drawing her closer, his voice low and deep. "Pay attention. This is our song."

But she could barely focus on the music because Marcus close up after starring in all her erotic fantasies this week was making her woozy with lust. The heat of him, his musky masculine scent, the hard muscled planes of his back under her hand, the gentle way he held her, guiding her in a sweetly graceful waltz. She was overwhelmed with sensations, her body's needs overriding everything, even the party. "How many dates have we had now?" she asked.

He straightened and pulled back to look at her. "I figure this is date two. First date was yesterday's lunch. I don't think we can count the Knicks game at your place or lunch with my mom."

She bit back a smile. "Plus when we went over my business plan over takeout. Everything counts. We've definitely had at least three dates." He'd said it would take three dates before he'd go to bed with her. Priorities.

He danced with her for a few moments before leaning down to her ear, his words a husky rumble. "So you remember what I said about three dates. The question is, are you prepared to adore me and only me?"

She gulped, not used to expressing her feelings out loud,

especially with a man. It made her vulnerable, something she never wanted to be. Like a turtle exposing her soft underbelly.

"Lexi?"

Her eyes unexpectedly welled. Oh, fuck. She wrapped her arms around his neck and hugged him, hiding her embarrassing cry face against his chest.

"Aw, Lex." He rubbed her back. "Don't cry."

She lifted her head, meeting his dark eyes. She wanted to say so much but couldn't seem to find her voice. *Yes, I adore you. I think I'm in love with you. Yes, I want to be exclusive.*

He gave her a gentle smile. "Mutual adoration on an exclusive basis, then?"

She nodded. Her gut instinct told her to trust in this relationship, to trust in him.

"Excellent." He resumed their waltz. "Did you know that was exactly what I've been searching for?"

"No," she croaked.

He stilled and framed her face with his hands. "You are what I was searching for."

Her chin quivered and she panicked that she was going to full-out ugly cry, her face trapped in his big hands, but then his lips sealed over hers, and raw hunger took over. Yes! This was what she needed—mindless oblivion. Nearly dizzy with the hot rush of desire, her stomach dipped, and a low ache in her womb made her press close against him. Her fingers tangled in his hair, lost in the kiss. There was only heat and hunger, winding her tighter and tighter, hotter and hotter.

Someone wolf-whistled, and Marcus broke the kiss, his gaze never leaving hers. She didn't even care that her friends had noticed them making out. "Let's go to your place," she whispered. "I can't wait."

He ran his thumb over her tingling lower lip. "Let's go back to the party. Slow, remember?"

"What?" She blinked a few times, the words not making sense, her body still in overdrive. "What!"

He dropped his hands from her and gave her a serious look. "I want to enjoy our date here with our friends, then I need to take care of some work stuff, and then I'll see you home."

He was seeing her home? So long, Lexi? And work stuff? He must mean Ellie. He was reserving time after the party to see Ellie back to her apartment, playing her security guard. She supposed he expected her to tag along and then let him play the same role for her, seeing her safely home. She was the last thing on his list of things to do. Not do was more like it. Either way, it kinda sucked.

She backed up a step. She just needed some personal space to cool off a bit. Nothing was happening tonight, and she was trying to reconcile herself to another chaste good-night kiss. Not easy with all she was feeling both physically and emotionally. She wanted him way too much.

He moved with her, a dark gleam in his eye.

She slowly backed up another step, working on looking casual about it.

He followed, his slow step purposely mirroring hers.

She threw her hands up. "Why do I feel like you're hunting me?"

He barked out a laugh. "Because I separated you from the herd. You're a lone antelope and I—" his words ran hot over her lips "—am a lion who hasn't hunted in a very long time." The look in his eyes was clear—hungry, determined, closing in for the kill. He wanted to devour her. Slowly.

Her breath hitched, the blood roaring in her ears. Her limbs were heavy, her body primed for surrender, hot and wet, aching to join with him.

He straightened abruptly, taking her hand and tucking it into the crook of his arm. "Now let's go back to the party." He led her back toward their friends, and she followed on shaky legs.

He stopped abruptly after a few steps, cupped the back of her neck and pulled her close, whispering in her ear, "While we're getting to know each other, here's something you might not know about me. I can give you G-spot ecstasy like you never knew existed."

She clutched his arm, throbbing at the words. Most men

could barely find the obvious pleasure spot, let alone the hidden trigger. Only her vibrator could do that for her. To have Marcus leading her there, bringing her to ecstasy like she *never knew existed* made her crazy to have him.

He pulled back and gave her a sexy knowing look. Then he peeled her hand off his arm. "Come on, bro. Time to get your ass kicked in pool."

She stared at him, speechless. Really? He was going back to the bro thing? Now?

He laughed, took her hand, and dragged her back to their friends.

She never quite recovered, losing in pool like she'd never played before. So freaking embarrassing. He had her in the palm of his hand and he was toying with her, being all friendly-like and not touching her.

Two hours later, as the party was winding down, she made up her mind. She was going to see this thing through all the way to naked town. She'd make it happen or die an unsatisfied horny death trying. She told Hailey she'd be staying behind and said goodbye to her friends.

Finally everyone left, and it was just the two of them. Marcus was behind the bar, putting things away.

She sat on a bar stool across from him. "I'm going home with you."

He raised a brow, but kept working, tucking glasses away. He wasn't moving fast enough for her taste. She walked around behind the bar and right into his personal space. He shifted away, moving to a sink and washing his hands.

This infuriated her for reasons he very well knew, teasing her with that G-spot ecstasy stuff and then completely backing off like she was just a buddy.

"I'm serious!" she exclaimed.

His lips curved into a sexy smile as he rinsed and dried his hands with a paper towel. Finally, he met her eyes. "Sure sounds that way."

She threw herself at him, wrapping her arms around his neck and going up on tiptoe for a kiss. His lips remained frustratingly out of reach. He was so much taller she needed him to bend.

His arms wrapped lightly around her waist. His smile bordered on smug, but she was too horny to care.

"I don't want to take it slow anymore," she said in what she hoped was a normal nondesperate voice.

"Lexi, baby, are you asking me to make love to you?"

"Yes!"

He inclined his head, grinning. And he still didn't kiss her! "Right this way."

"Kiss me," she ordered.

He laughed. "Aren't you something?" He tossed her over his shoulder like she weighed nothing.

The breath whooshed from her lungs, the blood rushing to her head, damp between the legs, all of her throbbing in anticipation. Now her dress was definitely leaving nothing to the imagination, bunching up around her hips.

"Beast!" she hollered.

"Beauty," he replied, caressing her bottom. "You're burning up for me, baby."

She moaned softly.

"I'll take good care of you," he crooned.

And she actually believed him, all of her softening, open to him body and heart. He stepped out to the stairwell, set her back on her feet, and surprised her, pinning her against the wall. His hard body pressed fully against hers. He lifted a hand, cradling her jaw, his dark eyes burning into hers.

Her breath hitched and then he kissed her. Aggressively. Fully. Possessively. The kiss went on and on—wet, open-mouthed, hungry. She wanted to merge with him.

He pulled away abruptly, took her hand, and led her downstairs.

Her legs quivered, her insides wound tight, all of her aching for more. This was *on*.

10

"Hey, boss," Ellie said, greeting Marcus the moment they appeared downstairs.

Lexi clenched her teeth. *Cock-block.* Or whatever the version was for women. Orgasm-block? Her lust dove to negative temperatures.

Ellie stretched her arms over her head, lifting her boobs and exposing her midriff. "I'm so beat, but I was too creeped out to go home without you. My ex was here tonight."

How much danger could the woman be in? She literally lived next door.

Marcus rubbed the back of his neck. "Give me a few minutes, Lexi. I'm going to see her home."

"Sure." *And I'll see myself home.* He'd wound her up all night and then he so easily turned from her to take care of another woman. She didn't want to be like that, but there it was. She was peeved.

Ellie beamed a smile at Marcus and headed toward the back of the bar, with Marcus following behind.

Lexi didn't wait around, heading in the opposite direction to the front door. Her hand had just connected with the door-knob when she was suddenly yanked back from it, a strong arm around her waist. "Hey!"

Marcus's voice rumbled in her ear. "I thought you might

bail. Come on, walk with me to Ellie's place, and then we'll go to my place."

She pushed at his arm, a steel band of muscle holding her hostage. He turned her to face him and held her by the shoulders. "I want you, only you."

The tension left her body. He understood her fears over men who couldn't be trusted and took the time to reassure her. She kept her voice low. "Could you ask someone else to walk her home?"

"Yes." A determined gleam in his eye was the only warning she got before he plucked her off the ground by the waist and deposited her on a bar stool. "Do not move," he ordered.

"Thank you."

He shoved a hand through his hair, looking around the bar. "Women," he muttered before disappearing through the employees-only door.

Ellie flounced over to the bar. "Where's he going?"

Lexi lifted one shoulder. "I think he forgot something."

"He's such a great boss," Ellie said, looking at her manicured red nails. "He really looks out for me, for everyone, really."

"Glad to hear it."

"Isn't The Burrow great?" She didn't wait for a reply. "I've been working here since it opened. A lot of bars fail in their first year, but Marcus got us off to a flying start. It's been big tips and pay bumps ever since."

"He's smart. I'm not at all surprised to hear it."

Ellie sighed and pulled out her phone.

Lexi hopped off the barstool the moment Marcus appeared with a guy wearing a hairnet. Marcus closed the distance between them, his hand closing over hers as he spoke to Ellie. "Mike will walk you home. Your alarm system will be installed tomorrow. Goodnight." His hand went to the small of Lexi's back, guiding her to the front door. "Now where were we?"

She glanced over her shoulder at Ellie walking toward the

back of the bar, Mike following behind. "Ellie sure sings your praises."

Marcus held the door open for her and followed her out. "I don't want to talk about Ellie."

"What do you want to talk about?"

"How about what you sound like when you're coming?"

"Marcus!" She glanced around the sidewalk. No one was close enough to hear.

He chuckled, low and deep. "Maybe you could just show me." He stopped walking, tipped her chin up, and kissed her. "I adore you; you adore me. We're exclusive, so now we can enjoy some of that exclusive-couple stuff." He searched her features. "Or I could drive you home."

"Are you crazy? You've been teasing me all night. If it weren't for that cock-block Ellie, I would already be in your bed."

His lips curved into a sexy smile. And then they were kissing, the heat igniting once more.

He broke the kiss, grabbed her hand, and walked so fast she had to practically run to keep up.

"Where's the fire?" she teased.

"In my pants."

Lexi followed Marcus upstairs to his condo on the top two floors of a brownstone, her fingers entwined with his, her pulse thrumming through her with excitement. He turned on the lights in the living room, revealing modern Scandinavian-style furniture. A tan leather sofa on a wooden frame, glass coffee table curved like a comma, and brown leather chaise lounge were set on a warm jewel-toned geometric-shaped rug. Hardwood floors throughout the space. Not the bachelor pad she'd expected.

He turned to her. "Want a drink?"

She shook her head. "Bedroom, mister. No more stalling."

He chuckled. "Right this way."

She followed him upstairs to his bedroom with a king-sized platform bed on a gray wooden frame, matching night-stands, and dresser. He turned on the white-shaded night-stand light, leaving it on a dimmed setting that gave off a warm glow.

She patted the cream-colored comforter. "So this is where the magic happens."

His arms wrapped around her. "The magic hasn't happened in a long time. I was waiting for someone special." He cradled her face in both hands. "I was waiting for you."

Her eyes got hot and she closed them, hoping he hadn't noticed. His lips met hers in a tender kiss. She wrapped her arms around his neck, pressing her body fully against his, reveling in his taste, his scent, his hard masculine planes.

His mouth moved over hers as his hands caressed her, sliding up her back and over her shoulders, down her arms, sliding to her ass and then to the hem of her dress, which he lifted. He broke the kiss, pulling her dress up and over her head, helping her arms through the long sleeves.

His dark eyes raked over her body in a black push-up bra and matching thong. "My God, you are beautiful."

For that brief moment she actually felt beautiful. Normally she felt self-conscious because she wasn't busting with curves like most men liked. Her ex had said she had less than a handful, which was why she had so many push-up bras. She shoved her ex from her mind as Marcus licked his lips, staring at her modest cleavage.

"Thank you," she said softly.

He grunted in response, stripping quickly, his fingers swift and sure on the buttons of his shirt. She watched with avid interest as more tanned skin and muscular chest were revealed. Then the shirt was off and she looked her fill at the most beautiful man she'd ever seen, from his broad shoulders to muscular pecs and abs. His dark happy trail led to a massive bulge. She reached for his belt, but he pushed her hands away.

He met her eyes. "Gotta ease the pants off when I've got a blue steeler like this."

She grinned, very pleased to hear the effect she had on

him. He eased his pants over his erection, down, and off. Her mouth went dry. "Full monty, baby," she said, staring pointedly at the tent in his black boxer briefs.

"That is protection." He grabbed her by the waist, lifting her for his kiss. She wrapped her arms and legs around him, returning the kiss passionately, his erection applying delicious pressure through the silk thong, making her crazy.

He lowered her to the bed, positioning himself over her as he kissed her, giving her only part of his weight. She ran her hands all over his warm skin, reveling in the heat and size of him. He broke the kiss, kneeling between her legs and pulling her to sit up. He undid her bra and tossed it. Before she could have even a brief moment of worry about the size of her breasts, his hands were there, cupping them, caressing, his lips nuzzling and nipping along her jaw.

She moaned. "Now, Marcus."

He whispered in her ear, "This is going to be slow, baby. I want to savor you." He then proceeded to make good on his promise, lowering her back to the mattress, taking his time kissing his way from her ear to her jaw to her throat, stopping frequently to return to her mouth—deep drugging kisses—his big hands continually caressing her.

"Marcus," she moaned over and over, her hands gripping his shoulders, smoothing over his muscular back, wishing she could hurry him up, but the man was determined.

By the time his mouth closed over one breast, her hips jerked off the mattress. He drew on her deeply, his hand caressing her other breast.

Oh, God. She was already close, her insides tightening with each deep suck of his mouth. *Now.* She smacked his shoulder, and he lifted his head, his lips wet, his dark eyes hot on hers.

"Put your hands under your head and don't move," he ordered.

"I want you so bad," she whispered.

"And you'll have me," he growled, "but first I get to savor you. Hands under your head."

Still she hesitated. She wasn't used to just lying back, letting the man do everything.

"Lexi, baby, just do it. I promise it'll be worth it."

"Are you going to give me G-spot ecstasy like I never imagined?" That was the only way she'd agree. Otherwise, she just wanted to get on with it.

His voice was rough and gravelly. "I'll give it to you."

A shiver went through her and she rested her hands under her head, which made her breasts lift. He licked his lips, caressing both of her breasts, his thumbs stroking the hard peaks. She moaned, her hips moving restlessly under him.

He lifted one breast, cupping it from underneath, his tongue flicking rapidly back and forth over the peak. She couldn't help her moans, and when his mouth finally closed over her, drawing deep, the hollows of his cheeks beautiful, she nearly came right there. He lingered on her breasts for a long time, caressing, sucking, tugging on her nipples, making her wetter, throbbing for his attention lower. She might have begged shamelessly.

She let out a breath of relief when he finally shifted, kissing his way down her body, his hands sliding over her hips and to the inside of her legs, slowly stroking upward, until her hips were off the mattress, so wired and needy she couldn't help but offer herself. He pressed her flat on the mattress with one big hand on her hip and then used both hands to spread her legs wide. She sucked in air.

His eyes locked on hers as he slowly lowered his head, his tongue taking one long lap over her.

"Marcus!" she cried, grabbing his head, her fingers gripping his hair.

He lapped at her again and then he made her crazy, stroking her with his fingers until she was trembling.

"Now," she ordered.

He stopped.

"Marcus!" she hollered. "Stop fucking around and fuck me!"

He smirked before lowering his head between her legs, his mouth taking over where his fingers had left off, only not enough, not nearly enough. Soft kisses, lazy strokes of his tongue. She writhed under him, desperate for more. His big hand clamped over her hip, stilling her, his mouth wicked. She ignited, each stroke of his tongue, every hungry kiss bringing an electric surge of pleasure. He brought her to the edge so many times she lost the power of speech, reduced to a low keening moan through the haze of sensations.

He kissed the inside of her leg, stroking her lazily with one finger, jolting her overly sensitized body. "Ready?"

She lifted her head off the pillow to stare at him incredulously. "Yes!"

"Lie back and relax, baby."

She dropped her head back on the pillow, so desperate for what he could give that she immediately complied. His head lowered between her legs, sucking gently. She moaned long and low. And then his fingers slid inside her, curled, and pressed.

"Ah!" Sharp pleasure speared through her as he hit the G-spot perfectly. "Oh God, Marcus, Marcus, Marcus." His dark head between her legs, his mouth working its magic, his fingers massaging her G-spot over and over and over, she lost it. The pleasure carried her out of her mind to a dark pulsing need, coiling tight, her body clenching around him, drenched with desire.

She whimpered incoherently, jerked, and then she came hard, bucking wildly against him. Sensation radiated outward like a starburst through her entire body.

And he didn't stop.

"Marcus," she moaned, shoving his shoulder, "I came."

He lifted his head, his lips wet with her, his fingers still stroking her G-spot, the sensations jolting her, making her hips jerk helplessly against him. She panted, on fire from his touch.

Their gazes locked, an understanding passing between them.

He owns me.

She trembled all over as he spoke soothingly, his fingers continuing to work her, pushing her for more. "Second time will be more powerful. This is what I promised you. Relax."

She let out a shaky breath and complied. He gave her a

wicked smile before diving back in, his mouth hungry, his fingers knowing and sure. A dark haze of pleasure consumed her.

She was going to die. Her body was in overdrive, sweating, trembling, at his mercy. His touch was electric, deep inside, her body bowing off the mattress, which only offered her up for more from his mouth, sucking, lapping, kissing, like he couldn't get enough of her. Her vision dimmed, Marcus's dark head a shadow between her legs, the room a blur, her ears ringing.

Her head arched back in a silent scream as the pleasure crashed over her in a monster orgasm that stole her breath, endless shockwaves of pleasure rocking her before she collapsed, the room suddenly black.

Her eyes fluttered open as Marcus stroked her sweaty hair back from her face.

He grinned, his head hovering over hers. "You passed out."

She slowly blinked. "I did?"

"I take it you liked it."

"Oh my God. I thought I was going to die."

"I took you to heaven."

She kissed him. "You did. That was amazing."

"You ready for more? Condom is on."

"Oh God."

"Oh Marcus."

She laughed and then she stopped laughing as he fit himself between her legs and slid inside. She was still so revved from before that sensation rippled through her with each sure thrust.

His fingers entwined with hers, pressing their joined hands to the mattress. His dark gaze was intent on hers. "Beautiful. You have no idea how beautiful you look right now."

She closed her eyes, overwhelmed by his sweetness, lost in pleasure once again. His thrusts accelerated, deeper, harder, until she was grabbing him by the shoulders, hanging on for a wild ride as his powerful body pumped into her.

"Marcus!" Her body squeezed him rhythmically with the intense orgasm, her hips bucking under him.

He let go with a roar, his head arching back, pumping over and over, bringing her more pleasure, her body taking everything he offered greedily, completely at one with him. Finally he stilled, buried deep inside her, the only sound their harsh breaths.

He lifted his hand, cradled her jaw, and kissed her tenderly.

She let out a swoony sigh, rocked body and soul. He was magnificent.

He rolled off her. She flung her arms to her sides in complete abandon, one arm thrown across his chest, totally and completely satisfied. So worth the wait.

11

Marcus lay on his side, admiring a naked Lexi on the mattress next to him. She was slick with sweat, her muscles lax, her arms flung wide open. He loved seeing her like this, open and spent. This was the point when most women left, sometimes on their own, sometimes he offered to walk them home. Not this woman and he'd make sure of that. It was one thing for her to admit she adored him, another thing to actually stick.

She was something, strong yet soft in all the right ways. He'd pushed her hard, wanting to bring her the greatest of pleasures. Not all women could get there, she had to surrender to it, to trust in him, and Lexi had. So beautifully and so completely that she'd actually passed out. That was a first. What pleased him most of all was having Lexi's trust. At least in bed. It was a start. He knew she'd been burned before by her ex, and it had been bad enough she hadn't been with anyone in months.

He brushed the damp hair back from her face.

Her eyes slowly opened. "Stop staring at me."

"Can't help it. You're beautiful. Stay the night. I'll make you breakfast in the morning."

She stared at him for a moment, her eyes soft before she looked away. "What're you making for breakfast?"

"Orgasm pancakes, you in?"

She laughed and relaxed again. "Who can say no to an orgasm pancake?"

"Exactly." He turned off the light and slid his palm over her flat stomach to the gentle curve of her hip. She remained completely relaxed, loose and limp, like he'd taken every bit of tension out of her. "So beautiful," he murmured.

"All men think a naked woman in their bed is beautiful."

"I'll tell you again when you're dressed." He pulled her on top of him and arranged the covers over them both.

She lifted her head. "I can't sleep like this."

"Why not?"

"You turn me on too much. I'm already getting excited."

Pure joy speared through his heart. He loved the way she spoke her mind. He shifted her, tucking her against his side. "Can you sleep like this?"

"No." She rubbed his chest, her fingers lightly tracing across his collarbone to his shoulder and down his arm. "You smell too good. Like sex and sexy male."

"That's a lot of sex."

"I know it. That's how I got here." Her breathing slowed as she drifted toward sleep. "What're you really making me for breakfast?" she mumbled.

"Cereal."

"I love cereal."

"I love—" Holy shit. He was *not* about to say "I love you," especially not first.

"Cereal," she finished for him.

He stroked her silky hair. "Yeah. Night, baby."

She sighed and then she seemed to be asleep. He lay there, eyes wide open, for a very long time. Had he finally found love again? He didn't know and could only hope that he was worthy of it now. Maybe this time his love would be enough.

So here she was in the bright light of day, sitting in Marcus's kitchen while he got out some cereal bowls. She'd worried about feeling awkward the morning after, but it wasn't like that with Marcus because he expressed himself so well she actually knew where she stood with him. Just this morning he'd said, while gently washing her hair with his big hands in the shower, "I'm glad you stayed. I'll never get enough of you."

She'd felt herself tear up, ordered him to kiss her, and he had. Then he'd rinsed her hair, placed her palms flat against the tiled wall, and whispered in her ear, "Don't move until I'm done with you."

The things he did, the way he just *knew*—

She shook her head, throbbing at the memory. She had to stop thinking about sex. She was never going to get out of here if she didn't stop lusting for him. Eventually he had to go to work, and then she supposed she'd take the train home. It was Friday and she needed to firm up the details for the Mardi Gras event at his bar next Tuesday. It wasn't just important for his business, but also for the potential to bring in future business for her. His bar attracted the Wall Street crowd, partly because he knew a lot of them, but mostly because his bar was conveniently located nearby.

He set a bowl of Life cereal in front of her with a spoon. "Voila!"

"So fancy! Any milk?"

He pointed at her. "See how distracting you are. You look so sexy wearing my T-shirt like a nightgown."

She smiled, starting to believe his words, especially when he looked at her like that. This gorgeous sexy man who could have anyone—she didn't kid herself about that—thought she was a beautiful sexy woman. He was shirtless, giving her a glorious view of tanned skin and bulging muscles, wearing only navy blue boxer briefs, which were tenting with a huge erection. *I made that happen.*

He leaned across the small breakfast bar, held her by the chin and kissed her. "I want you again, baby. Any chance you can stick around after breakfast?"

She nodded happily. "I've got a little time."

"I've got until eleven." He turned and checked the clock

on the microwave. "Two hours. How much damage you think we can do to each other in two hours?"

"Ooh, a lot."

He chuckled and got out the milk, sliding it over to her. Then he sat on the stool next to her, and they crunched their Life cereal in companionable silence.

She was only halfway done when he poured himself a second bowl. He shook the box at her. "More?"

"One bowl is plenty."

He topped off his bowl, took a spoonful, and chewed. "You're pretty sensitive about cheaters. I mean, I get that with my cheating ex, but was it recent or something?"

She swallowed. "If we're sharing war stories, tell me yours. How'd you find out she was cheating?"

He grimaced. "Guess I walked into that one. Okay, it's our one-year anniversary, and I've got everything set up. Took half a day off work to get all the ingredients for her favorite risotto. I spent hours making that and this coconut cake she liked. I also bought her a sweet diamond bracelet. Figured go big for the first anniversary, ya know?"

She nodded, already aching with sympathy because he'd made more effort than most men would ever think up.

He went on. "Then over our candlelit dinner, she says all sexy-like, 'What do you think about having an open marriage? We can still be married but, you know, take lovers on the side. Maybe even share some and it'll bring us closer.'"

She stared at him, shocked. "What's the point in being married if you're going to sleep with other people?"

"Exactly. So I say, 'No, I don't want that.' But I'm thinking to myself, how am I not enough? It's not like things got stale after a year." He took a deep breath. "So then she says, 'Well, our marriage already is open. I've got two other lovers, and I was hoping you'd be on board.'"

She gasped.

"Lex, I'm so stunned I can't even speak. Cuz she says it like it's just about being open. Not like she's cheating. So finally I stand and say, 'I can't believe you cheated on me,' and she says…"

Lexi leaned close. "What?"

"I thought you knew."

She leaned back. "Hell no! She puts it on you? Nuh-uh. That is just wrong."

Marcus shook his head. "I'm not sure how I was supposed to know. There weren't any obvious signs. I trusted her. Anyway, that was that. I packed my shit, filed for divorce the next day, and flew home."

She rubbed his back. "I'm so sorry."

He glanced at her. "Thanks. It sucked, but it was four years ago. I've moved on. Now when was your cheating ex?"

She swallowed. "Little over a year ago."

"Just one guy was the problem or…there's a history?"

She kissed his neck. "Hurry up and finish your cereal. I want to try something with you I've never done with any man before."

He gave her a knowing look. "I told you my story."

She hopped off the kitchen stool and walked around him to the sink, rinsing out her bowl. Only a moment later, his hand reached past her, turning off the water, his arms wrapping around her waist.

"Lex." His voice was a rumble in her ear. "I just want to know why you get so worked up about cheating. Sometimes it seems like you think all men are scum."

"Not all men," she said, turning in his arms and wrapping her arms around his neck. She pressed her body against his. "Not you."

He stroked her hair. "You trust me in bed. I know that, or you wouldn't let go like you do, but do you trust me out of bed?"

She dropped her hands from him and looked away. She didn't want to hurt his feelings because she loved him; she was pretty sure that was what this was. She'd never felt like this about anyone before, but the truth was…she just wasn't there yet. Her trust in men had been broken a long time ago.

He cradled her jaw, turning her back to him. "That's okay. I'll earn your trust, I swear. Just tell me why you think men are scum, me being the exception."

She grimaced, hating to out her family, but wanting to be as open with him as he'd been with her. "You're right. It's not just my cheating ex."

His hands went to her hips, holding her lightly.

She took a deep breath, staring at his chest. "My dad and older brother are cheaters. I never trusted either one of them because they lie and sneak and hurt the women who love them."

"Ouch."

"Yeah, not my favorite topic." Agitated, she wanted escape, but Marcus still held her by the hips, standing in her personal space. She lowered her lashes, unable to sustain eye contact. "I'm not used to sharing so much."

He kissed her gently. "I don't want to feel numb with you, Lexi."

She blinked back stinging tears. "I'm a little overwhelmed. I've never felt like this before about anyone."

He kissed her and then smiled, a wicked smile that stole her breath. "Are you ready to move on to the part where I blow your mind?"

"Yes," she breathed, throwing her arms around his neck and kissing him.

The rest was a hot blur, their mouths hungry, hands grabbing. He ripped her T-shirt off, leaving her completely naked. She yanked his boxer briefs down and off, stopping to drop a kiss on his hard cock. He jerked, which only encouraged her. She wrapped her fingers around him and then took him into her mouth.

He groaned. "Lexi."

She'd barely gotten started, turning herself on with each suck, when he pressed on her jaw, making her loosen her hold. He pulled her to her feet, lifting her, his lips sealing over hers. She wrapped her arms and legs tight around him, loving the feel of all that hard male.

Mouths fused, he walked with her until her back hit the wall. He ground against her, creating delicious friction. She dug her nails into his shoulders, soaked for him. Needing more, she held him, guiding him inside.

His head jerked up, and he shifted her so he could pull out. "Fuck. Condom."

She didn't let him go, her arms and legs wrapped around him. "Hurry and get one."

He walked upstairs with her still in his arms, set her on the bed, grabbed a condom from the nightstand drawer, and rolled it on. Then he pulled her out of bed in one quick move, already marching her backward. "I want you against the wall."

"Yes!"

He wrapped an arm around her waist, kissing her and guiding her over to the wall. And then he was lifting her, taking her in one powerful thrust, his arm behind her back to cushion her, fucking her and taking care of her at the same time. She hung onto his powerful shoulders, his thrusts sure and deep, rocking her.

His dark eyes gazed into hers as he slid a hand between them, stroking her, making her wild, bucking and clawing at his back. He pinned her still, pumping into her and stroking rapidly. *Oh, God.* The intensity skyrocketed, her breath coming in short bursts, white-hot pleasure surging through her.

She threw her head back, her body tightening around him, on the knife-edge of release.

His voice reached through the haze, gruff and growly. "You're trembling. Just let go. I got you."

She came hard, sensations exploding through her, hot and pulsing with life and love. Pure incandescent love. She pressed her lips against the side of his neck, bottling the words deep inside. His head arched back with his release, the tendons in his neck pulling tight. She bit gently on the cord of his neck and he roared, rocking her with his final pumps.

He breathed heavily for a moment, one hand on the wall behind her, one arm still around her waist, supporting her. Then he tossed her over his shoulder and palmed her ass. "Back to bed."

The blood rushed to her head, making her dizzy at the sudden change. "Yes, please," she managed.

He groaned. "We're going to kill each other."

She laughed, a giddy happy laugh as he gently set her down on the bed. "But we'll have fun doing it."

"Be right back." He went to the en suite bathroom, and she relaxed in his big bed, breathing in his scent in the sheets, his taste on her tongue still fresh.

He returned and smiled wickedly. "Now you're going to do that thing with me you've never done with another man."

"Oh, hmm…" That was, of course, a distraction.

He climbed over her, his palms on either side of her head, straight-armed, and looked down at her. "Let me guess, you made that up to distract me from our talk."

"Well…"

"Don't worry, I've got all sorts of ideas for you. You can tell me when we get to one you haven't tried."

She stroked his back, knowing he wanted only to make her feel good. It made her want to be more open. "Marcus, I-I almost trust you. Out of bed, I mean. I'll get there. Just give me a little time."

He kissed her, his fingers stroking down her throat. "Okay. I trust you, you know."

"That's because I'm very honest."

"So am I."

"Then just keep being honest."

"You have the worst beard burn on your neck." He shifted and rolled her to her belly, his hand sliding up the inside of her leg. "And right here."

She looked at him over her shoulder. "Totally worth it."

He stroked his fingers down her spine, bringing an electric tingle, before smacking her ass lightly. "Assume the position."

She lifted her hips. "Is this what you want?"

"Is this what you want?" he growled. And then his wicked tongue did wicked things and she fucking *loved* it.

Her world a kaleidoscope of colors behind her eyelids, she let go—

And she flew.

Knowing he'd take care with her, knowing he adored her, knowing, deep down, love.

12

So she'd spent the weekend with Marcus. He'd invited her to stay and then he'd made it easy for her, taking her shopping for a change of clothes and toiletries so she could feel comfortable at his home, giving her his laptop to finalize the event details. The S trifecta that was Marcus Shepard—smart, sexy, sweet—on full display. Swoo-oo-ny sigh. He'd driven her home on Sunday. They'd checked in on his mom, who was in good spirits, and then he'd stayed at Lexi's place.

Being with Marcus was easy. They just fit. She respected him. And she didn't give respect to a man easily. He was honest, open, and responsible. A man she could depend on. Probably the first time she'd met a dependable man in her entire life. His bad rep and the rumors about him just didn't fit with the man she knew. Most importantly, he wasn't a cheater. Yes, he'd been seeing multiple women at one time, but that was a reaction to his failed marriage, and he'd been honest with those women that it wasn't exclusive. He'd changed, and now he was with her. Exclusive.

He'd left her place early on Tuesday morning for a meeting in the city about the coffee shop that was opening in the space next to his bar. She spent the time on all the last-minute details for the Mardi Gras event happening tonight. She planned to drive into the city with the decorations. She'd tackle the setup and then she'd check in with the kitchen and the bar. The menu looked awesome—gumbo, jambalaya, shrimp with grits, and miniature king cakes. She'd found a bakery in the city to make the cakes and had them add a cherry in the middle of several of them. The person who found a cherry would win beads and a gift card to The Burrow. She was excited and nervous and hopeful all at the same time. Kind of the same way she felt about Marcus.

She stepped into The Burrow late Tuesday afternoon with three boxes of decorations that nearly obscured her view. She set them on the bar and looked around. The place was open, but nearly empty since it was early. Only one guy sat at the bar.

Marcus appeared through the employees-only door. "Lex, you should've texted me. I would've helped you carry stuff."

She couldn't help her smile. He actually took offense if she didn't let him help do stuff. Not only that, he made the bed each morning, his and hers, making sure there were no wrinkles in the blankets and fluffing the pillows. He was a manly man in touch with his feelings and quite domesticated—a truly extraordinary specimen.

She gestured toward the street. "There's more in the car. All the stuff for the activity stations and the prizes. I parked in the lot at the seaport."

"Key." He wiggled his fingers for her car key as he walked over to her, all masculine competence. So frigging sexy. "I'll move your car closer and bring the stuff in."

She pulled the key from her purse and handed it over. "Thank you."

He leaned down, smiling, and kissed her. "You can thank me later in your special way."

She grinned. "If you're lucky."

He laughed and headed out the door, saying on his way out, "I already got lucky finding you."

She sucked in air. Sometimes he just said these *things*, these amazing things that just *slayed* her. He pushed open the door, turned, and winked at her.

She ran to him, grabbed his shoulders, and went up on

tiptoe to kiss him. He met her halfway. "I'm lucky too," she whispered. "Go, just go." She shoved at his chest before he could see the tears in her eyes.

He was immovable. "Lexi, baby," he crooned, smiling with a soft look in his eyes.

She turned her head away, blinking back tears. He cupped her cheek for a moment and left, giving her some space.

She walked back inside, her hand on her pounding heart. She loved him so much it was crazy, like jittery happy, part scared, part thrilled. Her cheating ex had been the first time she'd had a serious relationship. All the other guys before him she'd been too scared to stick around long enough for something that might get serious. What she'd felt for her ex was nothing like this. And she thought maybe Marcus had deep feelings for her too.

She rubbed her forehead, belatedly wishing she'd invited her friends tonight, especially Sabrina. Her counselor friend could calm her and reassure her it would all be okay. She was sort of a love specialist. She pulled out her phone and typed a message to Sabrina: *I'm in love with Marcus.* She broke out in a sweat and deleted it. Just seeing the words made her adrenaline spike.

Focus. Fat Tuesday. Mardi Gras. Her brain blanked on her, all the details she needed to remember suddenly gone. *Overload, overload, overload.*

The event had to go off perfectly, and she was falling apart. She'd never done a solo event before, and the pressure to succeed combined with her roller-coaster emotions had her in a near panic. She needed Hailey, the ultimate planner, to help her through. Hailey had been working solo for years.

She sent a quick distress signal to Hailey. *I've got two hours until the Mardi Gras event and I'm freaking out!*

Hailey replied a moment later. *Do you want me to drive out there and help? I could be there by six thirty.*

Lexi's throat tightened. Hailey was such a good friend. And Hailey must be so busy with all her wedding planning. How did she manage to keep her cool with so many weddings and all those brides she had to shepherd through an emotional time?

Lexi texted back: *That's okay. I'm sure you're busy.*

I just finished up with a client.

Never mind. I got it. Thanks anyway.

Sure?

I'm in love with Marcus. DELETE. She took a deep breath in and out, and then she texted back: *Yeah, all good. Momentary freak-out. Thanks for being there.*

Anytime. You got this! Go, Lexi, go!

Lexi smiled, actually feeling calmer with her friend's cheerleading. She tucked her phone away and opened the first box of decorations—festive garland for the periphery of the room. She could do this no problem. Just focus on the event. One step at a time. She looked up to the high ceilings with punched tin tiles. She needed a ladder or a stepstool to reach.

She asked the bartender where to find one, and he gave her directions to a back storage closet. She dragged the stepstool out and got to work, starting in the front of the bar. She'd done half the room when Marcus returned with some boxes, setting them down on the floor.

"Lex," he boomed across the room, "I'm getting you some help."

She pressed the sticky double-sided tape in place and looked over at him. "I'm good."

He ignored her and went into the back. A few minutes later, he returned with two twentysomething cute hipsters she'd never met before. "This is Sara and Caleb. They'll give you a hand."

She gave them a friendly wave. Sara had long pink hair, a nose ring, and wore a black T-shirt with cutoff shorts and black tights. Caleb had curly messy brown hair and wore a short-sleeved blue shirt with white palm trees and brown corduroys.

Her new helpers jerked their chins at her with a friendly, "Hey," as Marcus watched them like a hawk. Seeming satisfied with their response, Marcus turned to her. "I parked you a block away. I'm going to get the rest of the stuff."

"Thank you!" she called after him.

He lifted a hand in acknowledgment and kept walking.

She sighed, watching his broad capable shoulders disappear through the door. Nothing better than a man who's got his shit together.

"He has that effect on women," Sara said.

Lexi stiffened. "I'm sure."

Sara nodded. "Everyone on staff has a crush on him, even one of the guys."

"That's nice," Lexi said evenly. "Could you find the box with the tabletop decorations? Caleb, maybe you could set up the long table over there." She pointed to where she wanted it. "Marcus said there was one in the basement storage."

"On it," Caleb said.

Sara lingered. "So you and Marcus are official, huh? He called you his girlfriend."

She felt herself flush. "Yeah, I guess it's official."

Sara lowered her voice. "Just be careful. I heard—"

"Marcus and I are good. I don't want to hear the gossip." She was past that. She knew this man, had taken a risk, and now she was in deep. She had to learn to trust in him.

"Suit yourself," Sara said cheerfully before heading to the bar for the next box of decorations.

Two hours later, with the event in full swing, Lexi was happily guiding people through the activity stations. Sara and Caleb helped her for the rest of the night. It turned out Sara was a waitress/artist and Caleb was a dishwasher/musician. They were really good with the customers, and she could see why Marcus would want them on staff. Marcus jumped in frequently to help and had done the white twinkling lights by himself, but he was also busy managing stuff behind the scenes, working with the kitchen staff, and jumping in to help with bartending.

The crowd just kept building as the king and queen of the bar contest spread through social media. They had twenty people enter the contest and put a poll on their fave social media hangout. Their friends were voting, sharing, and coming in to see the results. It was awesome.

Hurricanes were flowing freely, along with purple martinis made with blueberry vodka, and the fave of the night, the King's Cup, a champagne and vodka concoction in commemorative gold goblets she'd ordered special for the occasion with "Mardi Gras at The Burrow" printed on one side. The music was a cheerful Cajun zydeco. Later for the masquerade speed dating, she'd switch the music to jazz.

She stopped by the long table, where Sara was teaching people how to make floats out of miniature cereal boxes. "How's it going?" Lexi asked.

"Awesome." Sara lifted a small Froot Loops float with gold glitter and green feathers glued all over it. "This one's mine. I had to make an example."

"Nice!" Lexi turned to Caleb at the bar, who was egging people on to get more votes in the king and queen poll. He smiled over at her, and she grinned back. She turned back to Sara. "We'll wrap this station up in an hour and give out the prizes. Clear the table completely because it's going to hold dessert later. Everyone gets beads just for participating."

Sara grinned. "No flashing, huh?"

"No flashing. I'll get you a few necklaces to wear, and then you can hand out the others."

She glanced toward the booths in the back, where people were eating New Orleans-style food. She'd originally thought they'd do the masquerade speed-dating rounds in the booths, but there was no way she could kick people out of their seats. She'd just have them do the speed-dating thing standing. And it would be super speedy. Three questions, mark a yes if you were interested, first names only. She was pleased with the questions too and planned to eavesdrop as she kept the time for them. She'd asked Marcus a bunch of the questions earlier to whittle them down to the ones certain to have the most creative answers. The winners were: What superpower would you want and why? What would you buy with a million dollars? And what's your favorite cereal? The goal was fun and laughter, not a love match, but who knew? She and Marcus had bonded over cereal.

She danced her way through the crowd and slipped into the employees-only area to retrieve the huge box of Mardi Gras eye masks. She planned on wearing one when she announced they'd be starting speed-dating rounds for anyone interested. There were prizes too. Of course, everyone got beads, but she also had gift cards to The Burrow and some cute teddy bears wearing The Burrow T-shirts. Her goal was to bring people back to help Marcus build his business. She'd give out prizes for the cutest couple, most interesting speed-dating answer, and funniest. They'd have to voluntarily nominate funny and interesting answers at the end to win because there was no way for her to track all the answers.

She stepped into the large storage closet, pulled the chain to turn on the overhead lightbulb, and opened the large cardboard box, looking for the mask she wanted to wear. There was a really cute one that looked like cat's eyes. *Bam!* She startled as the door slammed shut behind her. Her heart raced. She whirled, fists up, ready to defend herself.

Marcus stood there, grinning. "You should see the look on your face—fierce and terrified all at the same time like you were gonna fight off an intruder. It's just a storage closet. Nothing of value to steal."

She dropped her fists. "You scared the crap out of me!"

"Sorry, I didn't mean to. I just wanted to see you for a minute. Climb up here and kiss me." He gestured for her to climb his body. He was a foot taller and loved to lift her up for a kiss.

She rolled her eyes. "Seriously! You scared years off my life."

He closed the distance between them, his arms wrapping around her waist. "How's it going out there?"

"Great. I'm getting ready for the speed-dating masquerade next."

"Give me a mask too."

She bent to retrieve the masks, and Marcus came up behind her, his hand sliding down her ass and between her legs. "Seriously, stop," she protested. "We're going to end up doing it in the closet, and I've got to get back out there. My boss is all over me to make this a success." She heard him—her boss—chuckling behind her and smiled as she retrieved two masks.

She put one on him with a gold and purple diamond-shape pattern and a gold fleur-de-lis right above his nose. Then she put her mask on, red sequins with black and green feathers around it. "What do you think? Would you recognize me in a crowd?"

"Might have to go by feel." He slid his hands up under her shirt, cupping her breasts. "Mmm…feels like sexy woman."

She shoved his hands away, her nipples beaded tight. "Look what you did."

"I feel terrible." He pulled her shirt up and licked his lips. "Let me fix it."

She grabbed for the button on his jeans, and he grinned. "I'll do it," she warned.

"Not gonna stop you. Have at it."

She shook her head and went up on tiptoe for a kiss. He gave her a long one that left her wobbly. Then he opened the door and gave her a little shove, following behind with the box of masks.

By the time the speed-dating round started, Lexi was flying high. She was in love, the event was going awesome, and everyone seemed to be enjoying themselves.

"Move to the next guy, ladies!" she hollered, resetting the timer on her phone. The couples were arranged around her: twenty-four single people had volunteered after much egging on from their friends and her tantalizing offer of prizes. She told the men to stay put and the women to move in an orderly clockwise rotation. The questions were a hit, inspiring some very creative answers and lots of laughter. She might even have sparked some real connections. She could under-stand why Hailey got off on this matchmaking stuff. It was fun to think you might've started a love connection. At least it was now that she had one, and also because it was voluntary. Hailey had stepped one too many times into aggressive territory.

She stifled a laugh as she heard a guy say he wanted the superpower to freeze time so he could have longer with his date. So cheesy! The woman groaned, and the guy quickly changed it to flying.

They went through the rounds, and she collected the cards to discreetly make the matches for further conversation. Next she presented the prizes, first to cutest couple, which was two people who couldn't stop laughing during their speed date, and then she asked everyone to report on what they thought were the most interesting and funny answers. After the votes were tallied and all the prizes given out, she gave everyone beads just for participating.

"You can keep the masks," she told them. A lot of them thanked her on their way back to their friends. A few of the new couples went straight to the bar for a drink and more conversation.

One of the guys from the speed-dating event pulled her aside, thanking her for a great night. He was in his thirties, his brown hair neatly parted to the side, his eyes a stormy blue.

"I'm Nate Kennedy, by the way," he said, offering his hand. The name sounded vaguely familiar.

She shook it. "Lexi Judson."

"Nice to meet you, Lexi." He squeezed her hand and released it. "Listen, my company is having a team-building event on Friday. You think you could plan a party for us after? Food's already taken care of, but I thought you might add something fun to celebrate our first year in business. Small office, thirty-person team."

"I'd love to. Absolutely." Only three days to plan, but whatever. A job was a job and she'd make it work.

"Awesome." He pulled a business card from his wallet. "Red Arrow Marketing."

"Okay, cool. I'll come up with some ideas and get in touch tomorrow."

He leaned close, lowering his voice. "I saw you earlier with Marcus. Don't be fooled by his charm. He's not who you think he is."

A chill ran through her. "What do you mean?"

"I just know what he's done to other women." He turned and disappeared into the crowd.

She took her mask off, going up on tiptoe to see where Nate went. He walked right out the front door. Strange. First he offered her a job; then he warned her off Marcus. She crossed her arms, hugging herself, a little creeped out. Why did his name sound familiar?

She went in search of Marcus, but couldn't find him anywhere. Maybe he'd stepped out for some fresh air. It was hot and crowded in here. She headed back to the kitchen to tell them to bring out the king's cakes for dessert. She had hundreds of them, way too many to carry by herself.

After she made her request in the kitchen, she took a box of the cakes out, figuring she'd stack them on the long table while she explained the game with the hidden cherry inside. She'd just stepped back into the busy bar when she heard Caleb holler, "The winners of the king and queen contest are Marcus and Ellie!"

She startled. She didn't even know they'd entered. She looked around for them, her stomach dropping like a stone. Marcus and Ellie were kissing.

Not a peck either, full-on lip-lock.

13

———

The box of cakes fell from her limp hands, her vision blurring through a haze of tears. She whirled, about to bolt, and then thought better of it. No, she'd done nothing wrong. She wanted him to know that she knew. She'd strangle him with her bare hands and then she'd go for Ellie. But first Marcus. He'd led her on with all his sweet lies! He knew how deeply she'd been hurt by cheating.

She saw red and darted forward, tripping over the cake box. She threw her hands out to break her fall, still managing to hit the floor partially on her face. *Ouch, ouch, ouch.* She rolled to her side, checking her mouth. Seemed to have her teeth. A coppery taste meant blood. She gingerly felt around her mouth. Great. Her bottom lip was bleeding.

"Are you okay?" a guy asked.

She got up, gathering her dignity around her. "Yes, I'm fine."

Marcus caught her eye. "Lexi."

She whirled and hurried to the ladies' room. She grabbed a paper towel with shaky hands, wetting it to apply to her lip. Her teeth had probably cut into her lip when she fell. After a few moments, the adrenaline drained from her, leaving her fatigued. She stayed in there as long as she could, pulling herself together by sheer will.

She would finish this event, head held high. This was an opportunity that could be big for her future business. She had a job with Nate, and maybe she'd get more offers at the end of the night. Otherwise, it was back to her parents' house or crashing on one of her coupled friends' sofas like a third wheel. Maybe she'd move in with Hailey and they'd grow old together, taking care of their fur babies. Fucking A! She should've known Marcus hadn't changed. All of her friends had warned her against him, but did she listen?

She glared at herself in the mirror. When would she learn? She'd taken a chance on him, opening her tender heart, and it bit her in the ass. She looked to the ceiling, blinking back tears. Then she just stood there, waiting for the bleeding to stop, furious with herself for letting Marcus get close. Finally, she tossed the towel in the trash, washed and dried her hands, and left.

Marcus and Ellie were waiting in the hallway. Fantastic. Just who she wanted to see.

"What happened to your lip?" Marcus asked. "You need ice." It was probably starting to swell.

"Excuse me," she said, the height of professionalism. "I need to go check on the cake situation."

"Lexi, wait," Marcus said. "Tell her, Ellie."

Lexi kept moving, not wanting to hear a word.

"Lexi!" Marcus hollered.

She made a beeline to the safety of the crowded kitchen. She could *not* have a big blowout breakup fight with him and keep this event going. That was for after the event.

She'd just stepped through the employees-only door when Marcus grabbed her from behind, dragging her back to him, his arms pinning hers to her sides.

"Let go!" she hollered, struggling like mad and getting nowhere. He was much too strong.

He spoke near her ear. "Listen. It's not how it looked."

"I am not talking about this right now! I'm finishing this event because I'm a professional. If you want to talk to me after, fine, but I have nothing to say to you."

He kept his voice low. "She kissed me. I didn't kiss her back."

She swallowed hard, wanting to believe but way too upset for a rational conversation. "I swear if you don't let me go right now, I will never forgive you."

He released her.

She went back to the kitchen, got some ice for her lip, and went back to work, pushing all the pain and anger down.

She finished the evening by handing out beads and her business card to everyone for any future parties or events they might have. No further job offers happened, but at least she had Nate. Maybe he had some kind of beef with Marcus, but that didn't mean she couldn't work with him.

She turned to find Marcus approaching, his jaw set, pure determination. Suddenly she was feeling so much more than irate jealousy. All of her previous doubts came flooding back. How well did she really know Marcus after three weeks of dating? Nate had warned her off: *I just know what he's done to other women.* Her friends had warned her off too. She'd ignored them all because Marcus had been so gentle with her, taking great care to make her feel comfortable. And they'd shared things, really talked. Was it all just a ploy to draw her in, make her vulnerable, and then crush her? Maybe every woman was revenge for what his ex-wife had put him through.

Her mind was muddled, her nerves shot, all of her hurting. She couldn't hold onto her righteous anger when she hurt this much. Everything in her screamed to put some distance between her and Marcus, but something held her there, some small part of her stupid heart that wanted to keep their connection.

Marcus grabbed her hand and pulled her with him.

Her heart raced, suddenly wary. "Where are we going?"

"To my office." They passed Ellie on the way. "Office," he barked at Ellie.

Marcus pulled Lexi into his office. "Have a seat."

She ignored the order, staying by the door in case she needed a quick escape. The office wasn't big, just enough space for a black metal desk, two folding chairs, and a file cabinet.

Marcus took a seat behind the desk, and Ellie took a seat in a folding chair in front of the desk.

Marcus looked to Ellie. "Tell her."

Ellie turned to Lexi and spoke in a monotone. "I kissed him. It wasn't mutual. I'm sorry if I hurt you."

"You can go now," Marcus told Ellie. "Shut the door behind you."

Ellie hustled out of the office, the door quietly clicking shut.

"Did you fire her?" Lexi asked. Her lip throbbed painfully when she spoke.

"No." He paused. "I know what it looked like, but nothing's going on. She misinterpreted our relationship, and I set her straight."

She stared at him, the pain rising in her chest like a vise around her lungs. Her protective instincts kicked in, the need to distance herself so strong electric waves of energy coursed through her legs, ready to run.

Marcus spoke into the tense silence. "I didn't even know she'd entered us in the contest. She shouldn't have done that. It was supposed to be for the customers. I had them draw another couple instead."

"She warned me away from you the first time we met. Obviously she wanted you for herself."

"That doesn't matter. Lex, you're bleeding. Let me—"

"I'm fine." She dug a tissue from her purse and dabbed at her lip.

"I'm sorry. It was never my intention to hurt you."

She swallowed hard, wanting to forgive and forget, but now everything was colored with the warning from Nate, alarm bells going off in her head. "I spoke to Nate Kennedy about a job."

"You got a job already? That's great."

"He warned me away from you too. You have quite the reputation."

His brows drew together. "I don't know why he'd do that.

He's a regular, but I don't think I've ever said more than goodnight to him."

Suddenly she knew why Nate's name sounded familiar. Ellie had told her before that Marcus dated Nate's sister and that Nate warned everyone away because his sister had tried to kill herself after Marcus dumped her.

"You dated his sister," she croaked.

"Who? I don't remember someone with the last name Kennedy."

"I don't know her name."

He shrugged. "You know I dated women before I met you. That has nothing to do with us right now. We're exclusive, remember?" His lips curved in a small smile. "You adore me."

Throat tight, her emotions tangled, she couldn't bring herself to speak of the ugly rumor. Maybe it was a lie. Maybe Nate had an ulterior motive. Ellie sure had.

"Lexi, talk to me."

She just couldn't open up right now, the shock and pain of everything that had happened too fresh in her mind. "Bye," she mumbled and turned to the door.

"Hold up. I'll walk you to your car."

She glanced over her shoulder. Marcus was standing, his brows drawn together over worried eyes. She wanted to forgive him, wanted to believe he was a good guy, but she just couldn't. Not today. "I'm fine on my own." He'd told her earlier where he'd parked her car, and now she was glad he had.

She rushed out, a little afraid he would stop her. He was definitely strong enough to prevent her escape, but he didn't.

One foot after another, lip throbbing, gut rolling, she made it outside, took a deep breath of bracingly cold night air, and went to her car.

～

Marcus drove to Clover Park the next day to talk to Lexi face-to-face. He needed to make sure they were good now.

When he got to Lexi's apartment, she wasn't home. He

pulled out his phone and texted her. Turned out she was on her way back to the city to meet with Nate. He tried to remember if he had a history with the guy, but couldn't place him. Maybe Nate was from his early Wall Street days? He didn't have any enemies that he knew of and couldn't imagine why Nate had warned Lexi away from him. The only thing that made sense was if the guy wanted Lexi for himself. A definite possibility. Last night she'd been the bright and bubbly life of the party, making it fun for everyone. He was already thinking about hiring her for more events.

He called her as he walked back to his car. "Bad timing. I just drove to your place, and now you're headed to the city."

"I'm on the train, so I might lose reception."

"I'll head back to the city right after I check in on my mom. We can meet at The Burrow when you're done with your meeting."

"I got a lot on my plate. I'll catch up with you later."

He stopped short. "Are you mad at me?"

"For what?"

"You know what. The Ellie thing."

"I'm sure you can't help it if women throw themselves at you."

He exhaled sharply. "I told you she surprised me. I would never cheat on you."

"Good to know." Her tone was dismissive like she didn't believe him.

"We should talk in person."

"I'll let you know when I get some time. Bye."

He stared at his phone. Shit. This was not good. She was blowing him off, he was sure of it. It wasn't just that she had a job to do.

Well, he'd step up and help her with her business. She had a solid business plan, and now she had some start-up money from his event. He'd help her come up with a cool website and put her in touch with his web designer. That would show Lexi how much he cared. It was the only thing he could think of to do.

He got into his car and texted her, offering his help. She replied: *I got this. Thanks anyway.*

Fuck. If she didn't need him for anything, how was he supposed to show he was worthy?

Maybe he should just lay it on the line. *Lexi, I love you.* He broke out in a sweat. What if she didn't say it back? What if she couldn't look past the kiss to the man innocently caught up in it?

He sat in the driver's seat, too lost in thought to drive anywhere. He mentally reviewed all of the facts. Ellie had said he was the king in her eyes, and he'd felt warmly toward his favorite employee. Smiling, he'd given her a warm, "Thanks, sweetheart." He always called women darling or sweetheart. Maybe he'd been too warm. Obviously she'd taken it the wrong way. He'd been so surprised he hadn't pushed her away immediately.

He hadn't realized Ellie had feelings for him. His intention with women was always a warm friendliness. Wasn't that what mattered? Intention? He didn't want to walk on eggshells around Lexi. He wanted her to understand that he'd only been friendly.

Maybe his love wasn't enough for Lexi.

And when had it ever been? His whole life he'd tried to help his mom, to keep her from being sad and crying so much. It hadn't worked. His mom got worse, having panic attacks for years.

His love was not enough.

Now she wouldn't even leave the house.

His love was not enough.

Even his wife, who'd sworn to love him and only him, had found him lacking.

Maybe...his love wasn't enough for anyone.

He rested his head on the steering wheel, a numb emptiness taking over, leaving him cold and tired. All of his efforts were for nothing. There was no way to fix this because it was him that was broken.

~

Lexi couldn't believe she'd gotten this new gig so quickly, but she was thrilled. Nate had emailed her with some of the particulars, including a small budget, but that was okay. It was her first real client. She stepped into the Red Arrow Marketing offices not far from Marcus's bar in the financial district. It was a cool loft-style open space filled with brightly colored chaise lounges, sofas, chairs, even inflatable exercise balls. Workstations were in the center of the space with glass offices around the periphery. Definitely a young and fun vibe in here. A young woman at the central workstation approached, wearing a cute light blue dress with daisies on it.

"Can I help you?" the woman asked.

"Hi, I'm Lexi Judson. I'm here to meet with Nate."

She smiled. "He's expecting you. Go right in. He's in the corner office." She gestured to his glass office.

Nate raised a hand, smiling at her. She waved back, crossed the large space, and joined him.

He stood and reached across the desk to shake her hand. "Great to see you again. Please have a seat."

She sat in a cushioned red chair across from his desk. "You too."

He folded his hands on top of his desk. "So, first things first. This is a party with food, beer, wine, champagne—all of that is already taken care of—but I'd also like fun activities and decorations like you did at Mardi Gras. Just so you know, the team-building exercise before the party is a creative one, where we have a competition to come up with the best campaign for terrible products. Just for kicks, you know, stretch the creative muscle and get some laughs. That's the vibe we want here."

"Sure, that sounds fun." She gave him some of her ideas, including a photo booth using an iPad with fun signs and backgrounds they could later frame and keep, a banana-split bar, and temporary tattoos of red arrows to show team spirit since that was their company name.

"Awesome," Nate declared. "You've got a real fun attitude and some very creative ideas given the budget. Ever think about doing marketing work?"

"No, actually," she said, surprised. "I don't have a background in that."

"We like all kinds of backgrounds here. It's the creativity that makes you a good fit."

Her eyes widened. "What're you saying?"

He tapped his chin. "Let's see how the event goes, but I'm thinking you might be a great addition to our team."

"But I don't know anything about marketing."

"You'd catch on."

She could barely believe she'd gotten a job offer like this so fast. "That's very generous of you, Nate, but I'm really enjoying being an event planner."

He smiled. "Then let's get you more of that business. I used to work for the biggest ad agency in the city, McCann-Thomas. Maybe I can pass along your name. As long as the party goes well." He winked.

"Thank you. And I'm sure it will go well. So would the party be here, or did you want an outside venue?" That was her biggest concern with the short notice.

He spread his arms wide. "We'll have it here. Plenty of room. I'll have some of the guys move the workstations out of the way."

She smiled, thrilled at how easily everything was coming together. "That'll work."

"Just one thing."

She pulled out her phone, ready to type in any notes he had. "What's that?"

His voice became hard. "Stay away from Marcus Shepard."

Her head shot up.

"No contact from here on out," Nate ordered. "You don't work for him. You don't let him near you."

She went hot and then cold. "What does Marcus have to do with anything?"

"It's simple, Lexi. Stay away from Marcus and you can have this job along with my glowing recommendation to McCann-Thomas."

"And if I don't stay away from him?"

His expression stormy, his blue eyes hard, he bit out, "Then none of that good stuff happens."

Goose bumps prickled down her arms. "Does bad stuff happen?"

"I'm afraid it will if you spend more time with him. I say this for your own safety."

"Why?" she whispered.

He leaned across the desk. "He nearly destroyed my sister. Her name was Grace."

"Was?" she whispered, horrified.

He straightened. "Some real twisted shit. First he tells her they can both see other people, but he makes her feel special. She's in love with him and she hangs on, hoping he'll stop seeing these other two women he was seeing. Then, finally, he breaks up with the other two. She's so excited, she thinks he really loves her and only her, and then he dumps her too."

That must've been when he was seeing three women. Stupid Marcus. Of course the women would feel special. He treated women nice. Well, except for the multiple-women-at-one-time thing.

"You said her name *was* Grace. Is she still, um, alive?" She'd thought she'd only attempted suicide.

He clenched his jaw. "She tried to kill herself."

"Is she okay now?" she pressed.

He slammed his hand on the desk, making her jump. "Everything was his fault. She changed her name and moved to Thailand. Last I heard, she was living on a farm. My family lost her. He destroyed a sweet trusting young girl."

"I'm so sorry."

"Don't you be sorry. It's his fault. Stay away from him for your own good."

She stared at him, torn between horror and sympathy. "Nate, am I here because you actually want me as an event planner or because you want to keep me away from Marcus?"

"Both," he replied coolly. "Now you have a choice to make. I hope for your sake you'll make the right one. Me or Marcus."

14

———

Lexi went back to her apartment later that day, her head spinning with all she had to do. She'd called Nate on the train and took the job. She had to. She was unemployed and needed the work. It was just one job. She'd made no promises regarding Marcus and frankly didn't know what to think. She'd calmed down enough to believe Marcus was innocent in the Ellie lip-lock, but this news about Grace haunted her. Had he ruined a young girl's life, or had the girl been mentally unstable to start with? Was he even aware that Grace had taken a bad turn?

This job would end on Friday, then hopefully she'd have a glowing recommendation to a well-funded company, and she could build from there. And how would Nate know if she continued to see Marcus anyway?

Did she want to see Marcus?

Her mind flashed to his mom, Lia. They'd become friends. Even if she and Marcus were on the outs, she wanted Lia to know she was still available to her if she needed something. So far Lia hadn't made any progress, not even to call the psychiatrist, but Lexi knew how important support and encouragement were for someone in the grips of agoraphobia. She called her just to check in.

"How're you doing?" she asked.

"Something's off with Marcus," his mom said, getting right to the point. "Is everything okay with you two?"

"I don't know. It's a little complicated, but I wanted you to know I'm around if you need anything. I mean, if Marcus is in the city or busy."

"I saw him earlier and he barely spoke two words to me. He's hurting, Lexi."

Lexi's breath hitched. They were both hurting, but she didn't want to get into it with his mom, which was why she found herself blurting, "The Mardi Gras event went so well I got another job this Friday. I need an assistant, and you're the first person I thought of."

"Oh, Lexi, I'm thrilled for you. I would love to help, but it's so sudden."

Actually it wasn't such a bad idea. Maybe it would help Lia take a baby step forward. "I don't live far from you, and I could drive you back and forth."

"Gosh, thanks, but…I'm going to have to pass."

"Well, anytime you want to stop by for lunch or whatever, feel free. I'll be working from home and would love the company. I'll text you the address. Or I could pick you up, no problem."

"Thank you, sweetie. Marcus is lucky to have you."

The stealth mom question hung in the air: *does Marcus still have you?* She swallowed hard. "Mmm-hmm. Well, I'd better go. I'm going to try a few ex-coworkers next. Just need a little help to get things set up."

"I so wish I could help."

"No problem. Maybe another time."

"Yes. Another time," she said softly. "Bye."

Lexi hung up and sent a quick text to Lia with her address and a link to a local taxi service if she wasn't up to driving. There. At least she could feel good about being supportive and encouraging to a woman who needed that.

She didn't bother calling anyone else about being her assistant. That had been an impulse invite meant to distract from the Marcus situation. She'd power through on her own and hire if she got a bigger gig. She pulled out her laptop and set up an online invoice system linked to bookkeeping software. Then she searched for where she could pick up the needed party items closest to Red Arrow Marketing and locally, trying to make it all happen in the least amount of trips. The online search sent her down another rabbit hole reading about fun creative team-building games. She liked to have alternate options for events whenever possible, especially if something went wrong.

By the time she looked up from her laptop, it was dark outside. What time was it? Wow. Past seven. She'd really been deep in work mode. She should get something to eat.

Her doorbell rang. Her brain morphed from work mode to panic. Marcus. It had to be. No one stopped by unannounced anymore. She checked the peephole. Yup. She pressed her lips together and got a painful reminder of her lip injury from yesterday. Was it only twenty-four hours ago she'd witnessed him kissing another woman? Mere hours since she'd heard about the devastation he'd wrought on a young girl?

She opened the door. "Hi."

He wore her favorite combo of sexy and badass—black leather jacket, jeans, and black work boots—yet she still needed some distance from him. "Hey, Lex, you eat yet?"

"No. I was just thinking about getting something."

He hitched a thumb toward the hallway. "Let's go out somewhere. Anywhere you want."

"Actually I was thinking of staying in."

"We'll get takeout." He clapped his hands together, rubbing them. "What're you in the mood for?"

She eyed him. He sounded wired, probably because of the way they'd left things.

"Lex, can I please come in? We need to talk."

She stepped back from the door, telling herself to try to be open despite all of her concerns.

He walked in, hands gesturing, his words tumbling out in a rush. "I realize you're sensitive about cheating, and I know it looked bad before with Ellie, so I guess the right thing for me to do is not be friendly with women at all. Would that fix this? No darling, no sweetheart, no smiling, no flirting."

Now she felt bad. He was trying to twist himself into some version of what he thought she wanted. What had Hailey said? The relationships that work out are the ones where the couple accept each other for exactly who they are. If she couldn't accept Marcus for the friendly flirty guy he was, then maybe she shouldn't be with him at all.

"Marcus, you don't have to change for me."

His eyes widened. "I don't? So we're good?"

"I'm not sure we're a good fit. You should be who you are. And who I am is a woman who doesn't easily put up with behavior that appears to involve my boyfriend with another woman, even if it's not actually cheating. It just makes me very uncomfortable."

"Lex, baby—"

"No baby, please."

"I can change—"

"You shouldn't have to. That's my point."

He threw his hands in the air. "So where does that leave us?"

She took a deep breath. She didn't open her heart easily and it would take time before she could do that again. She just needed some time. Then she remembered Nate's warning. "Do you remember dating someone named Grace?"

He stilled. "Yeah, I remember Gracie. Why?"

"She's Nate's sister. She tried to kill herself after you broke up with her."

He hissed out a breath. "Is she okay?"

"Nate says she left the country, changed her name, and hasn't been in touch with her family since."

He raked a hand through his hair. "And he blames me."

"He says she loved you."

His brows scrunched together. "She did? She never said anything. She told me she was seeing someone from her office while we were dating."

"Maybe she just said that. Nate says she was hoping you'd pick her in the end, and when you didn't, she lost it."

He frowned. "Jesus. I didn't know. Honestly, I never

would've guessed she was hurting. Gracie was always smiling, always happy."

"Because she was in love with you."

His eyes narrowed. "So now you blame me too?"

"I just think maybe you don't realize the mixed messages you're sending out, making a woman feel special without having much feeling for them."

He scowled. "Nate poisoned you against me." He pressed his lips tightly together. "So now we're through?"

She sighed. "Can you just give me some—"

"Time," he finished for her. "Sure. Take all the time in the world. I'm outta here." He stalked out the door and slammed it behind him.

~

Marcus stepped into his apartment and slammed the door behind him, furious with Lexi for turning on him just because of something Nate said. She only saw the worst in him. She wanted to see the worst because she was a man-hater. He'd thought that from the first time he'd met her, and what more proof did he need? After all they'd shared…

Hell. He wasn't going to wait around for her to make up her mind what she wanted. He'd be the one to dump her. He suddenly couldn't get a deep breath. *Calm the frick down. Think it through.* Facts. He needed facts. Fact number one—

His phone rang. He didn't recognize the number, but some sixth sense told him to answer. "Hello?"

A woman's voice asked, "Is this Marcus Shepard?"

"Yes. Who's this?"

"Jen Moore. I'm the one who found your mom collapsed on the sidewalk. We're in the emergency room of Eastman Hospital. She's conscious now and asking for you. The doctors say she might have a concussion. That's all we know so far."

Pure terror gripped him for a moment before he leaped into action. "I'm on my way."

He left the apartment, racing down the hallway. What was

his mom doing outside by herself? She should've called him if she was going to attempt her first outing in months. She had a serious condition. What was she thinking?

Lexi stepped into the hallway. "Marcus, I—"

"Not now. My mom's in the hospital." He brushed past her and rushed downstairs.

"Wait!" she called from behind him. "Let me get my shoes and I'll go with you."

He ignored her, running at top speed to his car. He got in, started it, and peeled out of the lot. Nothing could happen to his mom. It had always been the two of them against the world. He hadn't been there to protect her. Instead he'd been fighting a losing battle with Lexi, who'd turned on him. Obviously Lexi didn't love him. If she did, she would've heard him out, taken his side.

He rubbed his stinging eyes. Fuck. He couldn't think about Lexi.

He broke all the speed limits, roared into the hospital parking lot, and parked. Then he ran through the lot, through the busy emergency room, all the way to the front desk.

"I need to see Lia Shepard right away. I'm her son."

The receptionist took way too long to look up the particulars and sign him in. Finally, he was allowed back into the emergency room full of people on stretchers and in hospital beds with white curtains drawn around them for privacy.

He found her in a bed near the end of the ward, looking frail and beat up. The curtain was only halfway drawn around her bed. Her eyes were closed. Her right eye was black and blue and swollen, her cheek badly bruised with several scrapes, and she had a cut lip.

"Mom, I'm here."

Her one eye opened, the other nearly swollen shut. It killed him. "Marcus," she whispered.

A young woman in a T-shirt and leggings sitting on a chair next to his mom spoke up. "Hi, Marcus, I'm Jen, the one who called you. You sure made it here fast."

He nodded once. "Thanks for bringing her in. I really appreciate it."

"Of course. We're just waiting for the doctor to return to see if she needs some tests."

He stared at his mom, his gut churning. "Okay." He spared Jen a quick glance. "I got it from here."

Jen stood and touched his mom's arm. "Feel better, Lia."

"Thanks," his mom said softly.

After Jen left, he pulled the curtain all the way shut for privacy, though there were plenty of nearby patients and there was no real privacy.

He pulled the chair close, took a seat, and held his mom's hand. "What happened?"

Her voice was whispery soft like she was shrinking into herself. "I want to go home."

"What did the doctor say?"

She pulled the cover up to her chin and whispered some more. He had to lean down to make out the words. "I might have a concussion," she whispered. "They were talking about an X-ray in case I broke my cheekbone."

"How did this happen?"

"It's so noisy in here, Marcus. The lights are too bright. Can you take me home?"

"Let me check with the doctor." He stood to go, and she grabbed his arm.

"Don't leave me alone." Her eyes shifted nervously around.

He sat down again, his chest aching. She must be out of her mind with anxiety after being shut up in her safe little house for the past two and a half months. He brushed her hair back and kissed her forehead. "As soon as I talk to the doctor, I'll find out how soon we can get you out of here." He pulled out his phone and tapped on an app for a solitaire game. "Focus on this. It'll help you stay calm."

She started playing, her fingers clutching the phone so tightly they were white.

He went in search of a doctor. A nurse told him one would be with them shortly. Not good enough. He methodically worked through the ward in search of whoever had admitted his mom so he could get answers. Finally he found the right nurse and got the full story. His mom had attempted to take a walk around the block. She'd had a panic attack on the front porch, got dizzy, and fell down the steps. A passing jogger, Jen, had found her like that, bleeding and unconscious, and had called for an ambulance. Jen had been nice enough to stay with her. His mom had basically shut down, whispering her answers to the paramedics' questions and begging them to call him so she could go home again.

Why hadn't she called him for her first venture out? He'd purposely been living near home half the week just for her. Why wouldn't she let him be there for her? He wasn't enough. His love wasn't enough.

His mom wouldn't let him fix things.

Lexi wouldn't let him fix things either.

He was beyond aggravated. He was done. What was the point in trying when he couldn't make anything work out?

He returned to his mom, who was trembling, her teeth chattering despite the blanket.

"It's so cold in here," she whispered.

It wasn't cold. She was scared. It broke his heart. He took off his leather jacket and draped it over her like a blanket.

She relaxed a little. "I wanted to be brave. Lexi invited me to visit her anytime. She even offered me a job." Her voice cracked. "I tried just a small first step to go out, but I couldn't do it."

What the hell? He sat next to her and spoke as calmly as possible. "This is because of Lexi?"

"We're friends, and I think she really needed me to help with her new job. She said I was the first person who came to mind. She knew I was an experienced secretary, and we get along so well."

This was Lexi's fault. She should've run the idea by him first. He could've told her his mom wasn't ready to go out. At the very least Lexi should've been with his mom when she ventured out for the first time.

"You were very brave," he told his mom. "Baby steps. This is why I wanted you to call that doctor who specializes in issues like yours. You start with phone sessions and then work up to more."

"But I don't know the doctor. I know Lexi."

He ground his teeth, more furious with Lexi with every word out of his mom's mouth. "What was your plan? Walk around the block and then what?"

"I was thinking of driving to her apartment for lunch tomorrow. She works from home."

He closed his eyes for a moment at the terrifying idea of his mom driving and then having a panic attack, crashing her car. She hadn't driven in months. He leaned close, his voice urgent. "Mom, please get in touch with me when you're ready to go out again. I can drive you, walk with you, anything you need."

"I didn't want to bother you. You're so busy."

He straightened. "I told you I was living in town half the week. I made myself available to you."

"Lexi says you live just down the hall. I know she's the real reason you moved here part-time. That's okay. I'm thrilled. I hope by the time you get married I'll be up to dancing at your wedding."

A big assumption there, but his mom had always wanted him settled down. It occurred to him that Lexi was both the cause and the solution to the problem with his mom. Lexi had given his mom a reason to leave the house, even if she'd gone about it completely wrong. What was he supposed to do now? Lexi was done with him, and maybe he was done with her too. He didn't need this kind of aggravation. She'd really screwed things up for his mom.

"Can you get me some Tylenol?" his mom whispered. "My head hurts so much."

Shit. What if she had some kind of head injury? She'd hit it hard enough to lose consciousness. Who knew how long his beloved mother had been lying there on the cold sidewalk bleeding and bruised?

"I'll take care of it," he growled. Then he stood, yanked the curtain back, and raised hell getting a doctor over to her pronto.

Two hours later, he was finally able to sign her out with a checklist of concussion symptoms to look for. The doctor thought she was okay, nothing serious. Except every time Marcus looked at his mom's bruised face, her swollen eye, and cut lip, he wanted to howl.

The nurses settled his mom into a wheelchair—hospital policy—and he pushed her through the busy waiting room of the ER.

"Marcus!" someone called.

He turned to see Lexi rushing over to them. He scowled. She had no right to be here. This was her fault.

"Are you okay?" Lexi asked his mom.

"I've got a headache but otherwise fine," his mom said, speaking in her normal voice. "I just need to get home."

His mom was all whispers with him, but with Lexi she made a real effort. What was that about?

"I'll go with you," Lexi said. "Help you get settled in." She straightened and looked at him. "Okay?"

He clenched his teeth. "Go home, Lexi. I got this."

"Marcus," his mom chided.

He ignored the rebuke and pushed the wheelchair past Lexi and out the door.

His mom twisted in her seat, trying to see Lexi. "Go back and apologize," she ordered.

"No."

Lexi appeared at his side, slightly out of breath. "Marcus, please let me help. I care about her."

He couldn't yell at her like he wanted to in front of his mom, but all he wanted was for her to go away. He glared at Lexi and said in an even tone, "Let me make this easy for you. We're not a good fit, we never were, and now we're done."

She gasped. His mom might've gasped too, because it was damn loud.

He pushed his mom over to his car, leaving Lexi standing on the sidewalk staring after them.

Fuck it. He was done with Lexi.

15

Lexi gave Marcus a day to cool off, and then on Friday morning she tried to connect with him. She really wanted to fix things before she had to go to the city for the Red Arrow Marketing party. She was sure he must've stayed local, with his mom just getting out of the hospital.

Marcus was not making it easy—he wouldn't return her calls, ignored her texts, and didn't answer the door at his apartment. Finally, she decided to go visit Lia. Maybe Marcus would be there, but even if he wasn't, she wanted to check on his mom.

She rang the bell at Lia's house. The door opened to a scowling Marcus. His eyes were bleary, his stubble a dark shadow. Obviously he was worried about his mom, probably hadn't slept much either.

"Hi," she said. "I wanted to check on your mom, and I was hoping to talk to you."

"She's sleeping, and I'm done talking to you."

It was past ten a.m. His mom must be doing poorly. "Marcus, come on, don't shut me out."

He stepped out onto the small front porch, glowering down at her. "It's your fault she ended up in the hospital."

She sucked in air. "How is it my fault?"

"She says you invited her over *and* offered her a job, so she tried to go out on her own because she wanted to visit you. Then she had a panic attack on the front porch and fell down the steps." He crossed his arms. "She could've had a concussion."

"I had no idea. I would've helped her. I gave her a taxi service number and offered to drive her too. I thought visiting my place would be an easy step back into the world."

"She hasn't had a single session with a psychiatrist."

"I know," she said quietly. She'd encouraged her to make that call every week.

Marcus glared at her. "So she's suddenly supposed to be cured just because you selfishly lure her out?"

She tried to keep her voice calm, knowing he was lashing out because he was worried about his mom. "I wasn't trying to do anything but help her."

His eyes were hard, his expression stone. "She doesn't need your kind of help. So...don't come around here anymore. She's not your responsibility."

"Marcus, I'm really sorry this happened. There were no bad intentions on my part. Honest."

His lip curled. "As I learned with you, sometimes it doesn't matter what your intentions are. What matters is the outcome. Now she's battered and bruised, and it's set her back. She thinks this was all a sign she should've stayed inside."

That was an excuse. "She needs professional help."

He turned and went inside, shutting the door behind him.

She stared at the door. Now what?

She sat on the porch steps. Her only thought was that she should apologize to Lia. She hadn't meant to cause harm. She wanted to make sure Lia knew that. Maybe she could leave a note, but would Marcus let his mom see it? He might just throw it away. Maybe if she waited for a bit, Lia would wake up, and then she could text her to let her know she was here—

The door opened again suddenly and Marcus barked, "Go home!"

She jumped, her heart pounding. "What is your problem? I apologized."

He set his jaw. "Apologies mean nothing." His words were harsh, but his dark eyes reflected pain. He was hurting for his mom and probably hurting over her too.

She stood and took a deep breath. "I'm really sorry about your mom. And I-I want to work things out with you. I think if we could just talk, sort of clear the air..." She trailed off at the expression on his face, immovable, closed to her. She gulped and summoned every ounce of courage to put her heart out there. "Marcus, I love you."

"Love isn't enough," he muttered. "Not your love and definitely not mine. Pointless words." He went back inside.

Her jaw went slack. A thousand daggers couldn't have hurt more than those words. She whirled, tears blurring her vision, and rushed back to her car. Her eyes stung; her chest was tight, all of her cold, so cold.

She sat in the driver's seat, rested her head on her arms against the steering wheel, and broke down in tears. Time seemed to slow down as sobs racked her body, her heart breaking, hopeless despair swamping her. He'd turned against her. The one man she'd risked opening her heart to completely. Gone.

Finally, she had nothing left. No more tears, no energy, no heart.

Somewhere between her breakdown and her trip to the city for the Red Arrow Marketing event, Lexi drew on her last reserve of sheer grit and told herself there had to be a solution to the problem with Marcus. She was a problem solver. She just had to find a way to get through to him. That thin thread of hope was the only thing that kept her going.

The event went very well. Mostly because it was a party full of creatives looking to let off steam at the end of the work week. They were all pumped about their company's one-year anniversary too. There had been one embarrassing incident when she'd accidentally walked in on the female CFO giving a guy a blow job in the men's room, but Lexi had handled it very professionally, if she did say so herself.

The gender signs on the restrooms had been confusing or Lexi never would've stepped into the men's room. One had a unicorn sign and the other had a stick figure wearing a cape. Lexi had assumed the unicorn's horn was a phallic symbol and the other was likely Wonder Woman. Major tactical error. The CFO, Gina, approached Lexi later, asking for her discretion. Lexi swore up and down she could count on it. She was never one to spread gossip. Hell, it was a party. What went on behind closed doors between consenting adults was no concern of hers, and she made sure Gina knew that.

She stopped by Nate's office at the end of the party, where he was seated at his desk. "Hi, Nate, where would you like the decorations? You could probably use them for another party." The decorations were mostly large laminated red arrows on the walls and shiny metallic squiggles hanging from the ceiling.

He smiled. "Leave 'em up. It's festive."

"Okay, well, I cleaned up all the food and drink stuff. There's leftovers in the staff refrigerator."

"Excellent. I couldn't be happier with your work."

She smiled warmly. "Thank you so much. It was a pleasure working with you."

He took an envelope from his desk drawer and handed it over. "Here you go."

She reached for it, and he held on. She met his eyes in question.

His blue eyes bored into hers. "Would you like to have dinner tonight?"

She tensed, sure that the only reason Nate was asking her out was revenge against Marcus. Nate had been pleasant toward her at the party, but she hadn't gotten the sense that he was interested in her at all. Plus he seemed a little unstable.

She gave the envelope a tug, and he let go. She tucked it

into her small purse. "Thanks, but I'm with someone." At least she wanted to be with Marcus.

Nate appeared at her side, surprising her with the quick move. "Marcus?" he spat.

She eased back a step. "Yes."

He grabbed her by the arms. "You defied me! I said it was him or me!"

She tried to wrench herself from his grip, but he held her tight. "Get off me!"

He dropped his hold and shoved both hands in his hair. "Don't you know what he'll do to you? He'll destroy you just like he destroyed Grace."

"Nate, listen to me. Marcus feels terrible about what happened. He honestly thought Grace was fine. She said she was seeing another guy at the same time."

He leaned back against his desk, his shoulders slumping. "That guy was me."

"What? I thought you were her brother."

"Stepbrother." His blue eyes gleamed bright. "I love her."

Lexi's mind whirled, putting the pieces together. Grace must've had a different last name than Nate, which was why Marcus hadn't made the connection earlier. Well, this was all kinds of fucked up. She had no idea what to say, so she turned to go.

Nate called out to her, "You can forget about a recommendation to McCann-Thomas. I can't recommend someone who's with that monster."

She bit back what she wanted to say, *You're the monster screwing your stepsister*, and went with the far more professional, "Sorry to hear that." She booked it out of there. Like Nate's recommendation would be worth much anyway. Clearly the man had issues.

She burst out of the office's front door into the cool early evening air and headed down the sidewalk at a brisk pace. She mentally reviewed the entire event, especially her interactions with Nate, and had to conclude there were no obvious signs that things were off with him for most of it. Not until the end. She couldn't be faulted for choosing to work with him, but she certainly wouldn't again.

By the time she got to her train, only one thing was on her mind—getting through to Marcus. The fact was she loved him. He wasn't perfect, he fucked up sometimes, but so did she. So did everyone. And the important thing was that he'd tried to correct course, really tried to reach out to her and fix it. The past three days fighting with Marcus had been rough. He was everything she'd ever wanted in a man and never thought she'd find—honest, generous, kind, loving, smart, sexy, fun. Her eyes got hot, the lump in her throat painful. She sniffled and looked out the window as the train zipped along toward home, the familiar city scenery a blur.

She was sure Marcus would still be camped out at his mom's house. She'd text Lia before ringing the doorbell so Lia would know she was there. Surely his mom would let her in, even if Marcus wouldn't. She'd check in with Lia, ask Marcus to step outside for a private conversation, and then she'd spill her guts, telling him all the things she loved about him that made him the best man she'd ever met. She'd make sure he knew how deeply her feelings went. This was a once-in-a-life-time kind of love, and you couldn't just throw that away. She wiped away the tears that leaked out and took a steadying breath. She just hoped she could get all the words out before breaking down. It was so hard to open up, especially after his earlier rejection, but she had to reach past his hurt to his heart.

His harsh words came back to her: *Love isn't enough. Not your love and definitely not mine.* But it was. Their love was worth saving.

Unless he didn't love her back.

Was that what he'd meant? She crossed her arms, hugging herself, her skin clammy, her stomach rolling. Only one way to find out.

~

Marcus returned to work on Friday night mostly because his mom had kicked him out of her house. She'd said she couldn't stand him prowling around like a caged animal anymore. No one appreciated him. All he'd wanted was to take care of her, and she'd pushed him away. His love was not enough, never enough.

His staff stayed clear of him, except for Ellie, who found him in his office and reported on the goings-on in his absence. He listened, thanked her, and sent her away.

She lingered by the door. "You okay, boss?"

"No."

"Is it because I screwed up? If I'm the problem, I'll resign. You've done so much for me over the years, and I can't sleep at night knowing I hurt you."

He hung his head. "Stay. It's not you."

"Then what?"

He lifted his head. "My mom's not well, but there's nothing I can do. Lexi and I are over. Not because of you. Everything's just shit right now." His voice choked.

She gave him a sympathetic look. "Is there anything I can do to help?"

He shook his head and pulled out some paperwork. She took the hint and left. He went through some bills, a mindless activity he could do in his sleep.

His phone vibrated. He pulled it from his pocket and checked the screen. Lexi. Third time tonight. He declined the call, put the phone on his desk, and glared at it. She'd texted him too and he'd ignored it. They had nothing more to say to each other. He'd fucked up; she'd fucked up. They were a bad fit. Nobody's fault, really. It had been a forced arrangement from the beginning, two people playing at love. He didn't believe for one minute that Lexi actually loved him. If she really loved him, she would've believed him when he told her nothing was going on with Ellie. She would've believed in his innocence where Gracie was concerned. She would've trusted him because she adored him and only him. But she didn't so...fuck it.

His phone vibrated on his desk. He glanced over at the

screen, irritated, and then his heart was in his throat, full-on panic slamming him. He grabbed the phone. "Mom, what's wrong? I can be there in ninety minutes."

"I'm fine. Lexi's here with me. Now you listen up, this sidewalk tumble I took is *not* her fault. I don't want you breaking up with her just because she was nice enough to invite me over for lunch and to be part of her new business."

He looked to the ceiling, working on calm. Jesus. Now his mom was on Lexi's side?

"Marcus?" his mom asked. "Did you hear what I said?"

Deep breath in, deep breath out. "This *is* her fault. You weren't ready to go out, and she should've checked with me."

"The only reason I wasn't ready was because I felt uncomfortable talking to a doctor I didn't know. I felt more comfortable talking to Lexi." She lowered her voice. "She told me you're torturing yourself over me, and the least I can do is meet you halfway by talking to this doctor that came highly recommended just for people like me."

He dropped his head in his hand. "And did you?"

"Yes. Lexi and I talked to her together, both of us on the phone. We had a nice chat, and I think next time I can talk just me and Dr. Roberts."

His eyes teared up, so relieved he felt weak with it. "That's really good to hear."

"Now the three of us are going to have a chat. Lexi, pick up the phone in the kitchen."

He shot straight up in his seat. "Mom, this is a private conversation for me and Lexi."

Lexi's voice came through loud and clear. "Well, it would've been if you would've talked to me."

"Devious," he muttered.

"Damn right," Lexi said.

His mom chimed in. "I really like her, Marcus. She's A-OK in my book."

He rolled his eyes since his mom couldn't see him.

"Thank you, Lia," Lexi said warmly. "I really like you too."

He rubbed the back of his neck. "Do I really need to be in

on this conversation? Sounds like you two have all you need."

Lexi continued her conversation with his mom. "Lia, did you know Marcus is a big muscled mush of a man so scared to admit he's in love with me that he'd rather push me away? Very rudely, I might add. His exact words were 'go home!'"

"Marcus, really," his mom chided. "Haven't I raised you with kindness? Those are harsh words, and words matter. Now apologize to Lexi."

He ground his teeth. "I will not apologize."

"I'm not sorry either," Lexi said. "Not for one single thing."

"Great," he said.

"Do you know what, Lexi?" his mom asked.

"What's that, Lia?"

"I have never, not once, seen Marcus as happy as he's been with you. That is the truth. And the only reason I'm so motivated to work through this darn agoraphobia is because you told me how wonderful you thought he was and how very much you love him. I'm sure marriage is in your future."

Marcus shot out of his seat. "What's that now?"

Lexi spoke, her words coming out in a rush. "Marcus, it's really hard for me to open up, especially with a witness, especially after your rejection, but here goes. You are everything. You are…" Her voice choked. "Sorry, I-I…"

He gripped the phone tighter, the emotion in her voice so strong it hit him deep inside. She did love him. His anger, his hurt, all of his defenses against her crumpled in that moment. "Lex—"

"No, let me finish. I need you to know how deep it goes. You are honest, kind, generous, loving, smart…" She sniffled. "And fun and beautiful in your manly way, inside and out, and I'm spilling my guts here because I love you so freaking much it hurts. I've never felt this way before about anyone, and I don't think I ever will again. This is a once-in-a-lifetime kind of love, Marcus, and it's worth saving."

His eyes welled, his throat tight. He was about to agree when his mom decided to add her two cents.

"You can see why I thought for certain marriage was in your future. Lexi, I know he longs for that forever love, and I've decided you're it."

"Mom, please. Let me talk to Lexi."

"Who's stopping you?"

"Marcus?" Lexi asked in a strained voice.

He swallowed over the lump in his throat. "Lex, you're everything to me too. I agree with everything you just said." He wanted to spill his guts too, but it was tough with his mom still on the phone.

"That settles it," his mom said cheerfully. "I knew she was your future bride."

"I like that idea," Lexi said, sounding happy now.

Pure joy rushed through him. He cleared his throat loudly. "Excuse me, ladies, do I get a say in this?"

"No," they said in unison.

His lips twitched. They were a united front in their love for him. Maybe he was enough. Otherwise, why would his mom care so much about getting him back with Lexi, and why would Lexi care so much to go the embarrassing route of bringing his mom into the conversation?

"I love you, Marcus," his mom said. "Now come get your future bride."

Lexi spoke up. "Your future bride will come to you. Where are you?"

"I'm at work."

"I'll be there as soon as I can."

"Now hold on," his mom said. "Marcus, don't you have something you'd like to tell Lexi back?"

He stifled a laugh. "Mom, I'm hanging up now."

"Rhymes with dove," his mom offered, in case he was that dense.

Lexi laughed. "Words don't mean much to him. He's all about action."

His mom huffed. "Marcus Christian Shepard, get with the program!"

Geez, the full-name treatment. "I love you both," he murmured and hung up.

He left his office with a spring in his step. And he couldn't stop smiling.

~

Lexi took one step into The Burrow and was immediately accosted by Ellie. "I'm so sorry if I screwed things up! I feel terrible. I got carried away, and I guess I thought, wrongly, that Marcus had feelings for me."

Lexi studied her for a moment; her sincerity was clear, but still. "The thing is, Ellie, you knew we were together. I don't see how it ever should've crossed your mind that it was a good idea to kiss another woman's boyfriend."

"I'd been drinking," she whispered. "Please don't tell him. I know I'm not supposed to be drinking when I'm at work. But...I was jealous and it was wrong. I really am sorry."

"We're together now in a committed relationship. It's serious. Is that going to be a problem for you?"

"He committed?" Ellie whispered. "When? How? Did he propose?"

"Does it matter?"

Ellie bit her lip, her eyes shiny with unshed tears. "I'm going on break." She whirled, dashing toward the kitchen. Marcus appeared through the employees-only door, and Ellie veered around him without a word.

Lexi's eyes locked on Marcus striding toward her, a huge smile spreading on his face the closer he got. Her heart kicked up speed, warmth radiating through her, all of her lit up with pure happiness and love, so much love. She'd gotten through to him and he was coming back to her. He loved her.

He stopped short in front of her, legs spread apart, and slammed his hands on his hips. "So you brought out the big guns, huh? Went the mom route."

She grinned up at him and spread her arms wide. "You're a big guy. It takes a lot to bring you down."

He grabbed her, giving her a bear hug that lifted her right off the ground. She laughed as he spun her in a circle before setting her back on her feet. He kept her close, wrapped in his arms, his sigh parting her hair. "Tell me again."

She knew what he wanted. She lifted her head and met his eyes, the words coming easier now that she'd spilled her guts earlier. "I love you."

He framed her face with his hands. "I love you too so damn much. You're everything to me, my heart, my soul, my love." His words speared her heart. His eyes warm and tender, gazing into hers, sealed the deal. "You are the best woman I've ever met, so loving, so honest and straightforward, so strong, willing to fight for what's important, willing to fight for us." He dropped his hands from her face, wrapped his arms around her, and slowly shook his head, smiling. "You've ruined me for any other woman, so I hope you're happy. Now you're stuck with me."

She beamed at him, all of her awake and alive, exhilarated by her amazing man. She hugged him tight and pulled back to look at him. "Oh, Marcus, I'm ridiculously happy. And you're stuck with me too."

He kissed her. "I can't believe you said all that stuff with my mom listening in."

She shrugged one shoulder. "I love your mom."

He smoothed her hair back behind her ear. "I love that you love my mom."

She smiled cheekily. "Is that your favorite thing about me?"

"Nope. My favorite thing is that you're my future bride."

Her breath caught, her skin flushed hot, her knees weak. "I thought you were just agreeing with your mom's romantic idea."

"Nuh-uh. This is forever, Lex."

She slapped a hand over her mouth, her heart swelling, bursting with love for this extraordinary man who loved her and only her, so much he wanted her in his life forever. "Really?" she asked behind her hand.

He nodded solemnly.

She dropped her hand, biting back a smile. "So that's it? That's my proposal?"

He went down on one knee. "Alexis Judson, will you marry me?"

The full name! How formal! How gentlemanly! How adorable! "Where's my ring?"

He gave her a wry look, strode behind the bar, and returned with an aluminum foil ring he'd just created.

"Ooh! Fancy!" she exclaimed.

He took a knee and held the ring up to her. "Will you do me the honor of being my wife, adoring me and only me for the rest of my studly life?"

She laughed a giddy happy laugh. "I will!" He slid the foil ring on her finger. It was huge and gaudy. She couldn't wait to show her friends.

He stood and kissed her passionately, bending her back over his arm. Swoon!

He brought her back upright, smiling at her tenderly. "We'll replace that with a real ring this weekend."

"Are you kidding me?" She held up her ring hand. "This is everything! Spontaneous, romantic, and homemade by my studly man."

"You're a little nuts, aren't you?"

She threw her arms around his neck. "But you love me anyway."

He smiled down at her, wrapping his arms around her waist. "I do. Maybe I'm a little nuts too."

"Let's go back to your place and do dirty things to each other."

He held her by the chin. "You are definitely the right fit for me."

"That sounds dirty."

He threw back his head and laughed. "Yup. Definitely the right woman."

She beamed, watching him go behind the bar and grab his jacket. Once he returned to her, she informed him, "I never thought I'd be a bride."

"No? I thought all women dreamed of that."

"Now I will."

"I'm glad."

He held the front door open for her and she brushed past him, still secretly thrilled with his fine manners. He joined her on the sidewalk, entwined his fingers with hers, and they made the short walk back to his place.

"Lex, I gotta thank you for what you did for my mom. You really connected with her in a way I couldn't, and she's better off for it."

"You know, I think she was trying to protect you from her issues, trying not to bother you with it. Maybe she just needed an outsider to give her a little nudge."

He exhaled sharply. "Maybe. I just had such a weight on my shoulders, you know? I've been the man of the house since my dad died."

"Was he sick?"

"No. He was a drug dealer. He got arrested, offered testimony for a lesser sentence, and was killed shortly after by the big-time drug boss."

She squeezed his hand. "Shit. I'm so sorry. That's a lot of pressure for a kid. Is that why you're so muscled? You needed to be strong?"

He cocked his head. "Never thought about it that way. Maybe I just wanted to know I could protect me and my mom. Plus I like being in shape. It feels good."

She stroked his hugely muscled bicep through his jacket. "It does feel good."

He lifted her to eye level and kissed her.

She grinned. "I like it better when we're horizontal because we're on more equal footing. You're too damn tall."

He set her back on her feet. "Maybe you're too damn small."

"Our kids will be average."

"Lex," he said in a choked voice, "you mean it? You want to have kids with me?"

"Absolutely. You'd make a great dad."

He grabbed her in a hug and twirled her around. She laughed, delighted with his enthusiasm. He took her hand and tugged her along. "Come on, bed for you. I want to make you as happy as you've made me."

"That's a tall order."

"I'll say."

They made it to his place and walked straight to his bedroom. While he turned on the nightstand light and pulled back the covers, she stripped down completely naked.

He turned and swore. "So beautiful. Get over here, baby."

"Strip, stud, let me see those muscles."

His dark eyes gleaming, he stripped completely in all his glorious male beauty. She wasn't aware of crossing the room. One minute she was looking her fill and the next she was in his arms. And then they were kissing passionately, hands roaming, hungry for each other.

He guided her to the bed and set her in the center of the mattress. She opened her arms to him. He smiled, rolled on a condom, and then he joined her, settling between her legs.

She wrapped her arms and legs around him, so eager for this joining. He thrust inside, and they both groaned. This time was slower, their breaths mingling.

Marcus twined his fingers with hers and raised them over her head. "I love you so much."

"I love you too so much."

"I adore you and only you."

Her throat tightened, her eyes hot because he knew how to love her in exactly the way she needed. "Me too. Kiss me before I cry."

"Aww, Lex." His mouth sealed over hers. Time ceased existing. There was just this, the two of them merged as one, body and soul. She'd never felt closer to another person before, her trust in him complete.

A long while later, he broke the kiss, his breath harsh. He held her head with one large hand, gazing into her eyes. "More." He slid his other hand under her hip and tilted her up to take him deeper.

"Ah!" He hit just the right angle, the pleasure so intense her body tightened around him, milking him with her release. Her gaze never left his, held in thrall as euphoria flooded her body, heart hammering, breathless, electric sensations sparking through every nerve ending. He pumped deep and then let go, clutching her tight to him.

She held him tight, too, a surge of love so powerful radiating between them it made her hyperaware of everything—his heart hammering against hers, the heat of their skin pressed so close, his masculine scent, the flex of his muscles surrounding her. She never wanted to let him go, and then she relaxed, loosening her hold as beautiful reality sank in—

He was hers, and she was his. Forever.

EPILOGUE

"Two engagement parties in one week!" Lexi exclaimed to Marcus.

"Lots to celebrate," he said, walking her into Garner's Sports Bar & Grill.

She beamed at him. Yup, she'd officially joined the ranks of annoying lovey-dovey couples. And she *loved* it. It had been a whirlwind romance—three weeks to a proposal and another three weeks for her to move into his condo in the city. The move had been just yesterday. Hey, when it was right, it was right. They'd both been ready for a committed relation-ship. She still planned to visit Clover Park for all of her friends' special occasions, girls' night, and their Happy Endings Book Club meetings.

Today was Sunday, and the engagement party was for Brandy and Joe. Yup! Hailey's mom and Josh's dad were offi-cially tying the knot. Next Saturday she and Marcus would have their engagement party at his mom's house. Lia had planned the whole thing, and it had been an important step forward for her as she reached out to invite friends. She'd even gotten in touch with her parents in Florida, which Marcus was thrilled about because they planned on staying for a long visit. His theory was that his grandparents would either be great company or drive his mom nuts and she'd be eager to leave the house. Lia was making fantastic progress. She was keeping up her phone sessions with Dr. Roberts, had adopted a gray cat that she adored, and had also taken a few short walks with Lexi and Marcus.

Lexi practically floated over to the bar in her giddy happy state. Her life had fallen into place in ways she'd never expected. She was getting married (!), she'd helped Lia reclaim her life, and her business was off to a flying start. The CFO at Red Arrow Marketing, Gina, was so happy with Lexi's discretion regarding the men's room incident that she'd spread the word through her contacts that Lexi could be depended upon with delicate situations. Lexi had already gotten calls from some very high-level people, who valued discretion in their party planners.

Ellie was out of Marcus's life, too, and that had been her decision. The day after Lexi had told Ellie how serious things were with her and Marcus, Ellie quit. Not only that, Ellie had moved out of Marcus's rental and over to her friend's place in Brooklyn. She must've realized it was time for her to move on from Marcus. Lexi felt a little bad about how that had left Marcus scrambling for a good replacement, but she couldn't summon much warmth for the woman who'd crossed the line with her man.

Marcus took a seat at the bar next to the guys, and Lexi excused herself to go congratulate Brandy. Hailey was with her mom. She'd planned tonight's engagement party for her mom and Joe. Hailey didn't have her constant companion, Rose, with her tonight because her mom was allergic. Too bad because Rose kept Hailey on an even keel for the most part, except when Josh was around. Polite but cool was the name of the game between Josh and Hailey now. It had been more than a month since the Hailey-Josh fallout, and neither of them would speak a word about the disastrous night when Hailey had gone to Josh's place.

Lexi reached Brandy and Hailey, the pair strikingly similar —same long strawberry blond hair, pale blue eyes, fair skin, and a preference for designer dresses.

Hailey's back was to Lexi, and she was speaking earnestly. "I'm glad you're happy, Mom. Really."

Brandy took Hailey's hands and squeezed. "He's one of those rare men who believes in chivalry. He treats me like a queen! Opening doors, helping me into my chair, assisting with my coat, escorting me like this." She released Hailey's hands and crooked an elbow.

"Josh does that too," Lexi put in.

Hailey whirled. "Hi."

"Hi!" She turned to Brandy. "Congratulations."

"You too," Brandy said warmly. "Aren't we so lucky to be brides? I feel like Joe would slay dragons for me. He's a true man in every good sense of the word." Brandy winked. "And an animal in bed."

Lexi laughed.

"Mom, TMI!" Hailey protested.

"I thought we could talk like friends now that you're an adult," Brandy said.

"Yes, but not about that," Hailey whispered. "How many times do I have to say it? Boundaries!"

Her mom got dreamy. "He's so in tune with my body."

Lexi considered bolting on the private conversation, but it was fascinating in a car-crash kind of way.

"I can't even…" Hailey took a deep breath and held up her palm. "Let's please not talk about Mr. Campbell that way."

Brandy pouted. "Sorry. I don't have close friends like you do to share with. Just the ladies from the shop and they're so catty."

Hailey hugged her mom. "I'm so glad you've found happiness."

Brandy beamed. "Will you plan our wedding?"

Hailey pulled back, her expression tight. "Of course."

"I want you to be my maid of honor."

Hailey pasted on her beauty-queen smile. *Uh-oh. Stress level rising!* "I would love that."

Her mom smiled and walked away.

"You okay?" Lexi asked gently. It must suck for Hailey—

the love-obsessed wedding planner—to have all of her friends *and* her mom planning weddings when she wasn't even dating anyone.

"Sure, sure," Hailey said, patting her purse like she was looking for Rose. She suddenly seemed to remember that Rose was with a dog sitter, dropped her hand, and turned to Lexi. "Can I get you some champagne?" Ever the polite host.

"Sure. We'll both get some."

They walked over to the bar, and Josh greeted them with a polite but decidedly cool, "What can I get you ladies?"

They ordered two champagnes. Josh served them up a few moments later and rested his elbows on the bar across from Hailey. "I'm best man. Looks like I'll be your wedding escort again."

Hailey's lower lip wobbled. Lexi froze. She'd only ever seen Hailey cry once after ending a long relationship. Normally nothing fazed her.

"Don't cry," Josh said urgently.

Hailey burst into tears.

"Oh, Hailey," Lexi said, wrapping an arm around her shoulders. "It's okay. It's an emotional time."

Josh appeared at Lexi's side and took over, leading Hailey away. He parked Hailey in a back booth of the restaurant, her back to their group. Her shoulders moved up and down with her sobs. Josh dropped to his haunches, speaking quietly to her.

Lexi had a quick conference with her friends over intervening. Josh was handing Hailey napkins from the dispenser now. She shook a napkin, talking to him and crying at the same time.

Finally, they all turned to relationship counselor Sabrina for her expert opinion.

"Let Josh do his thing," Sabrina said. "She's the last single woman in our group; even her mom beat her to it. Given how much she loves love—"

"She calls herself the Love Junkie," Mad put in.

Sabrina went on. "This is a difficult adjustment. She just needs some time to process."

Hailey was shaking her head at something Josh was saying, her voice rising, but not enough to make out her words.

"Should we go over there now?" Lexi asked.

Marcus appeared at her side. "Rescue is his specialty. He'll come through."

"Yeah, let it play out," Mad said. "She'll walk away if he's not being helpful. Honestly Josh always comes through in difficult times. There's no better person you want on your side." Josh was Mad's big brother, so she would know.

They all watched as Josh guided Hailey toward the kitchen in the back of the restaurant, a hand on the small of her back. Hailey let her hair hang in her face, hiding her tears, her shoulders hunched. Maybe Josh was leading her to a more private space, or maybe they'd leave through the back exit.

Mad stared after them. "She can't leave. She's the host of her mom's party."

"Don't you wonder what they're saying?" Lexi asked.

Mad twisted her lips to the side. "She's saying her love life sucks."

Lexi added Josh's side. "He's saying don't worry about it, so does mine."

Marcus chimed in. "Eventually they'll draw the conclusion that solves both of their problems."

"Don't be so sure," Lexi and Mad said at the same time. Their friends were in agreement. It wasn't a sure thing at all with those two.

Marcus pulled Lexi close, his voice a husky rumble in her ear. "Thankfully, I got you locked down."

She looked up at him, smiling. "You do, huh?"

He gave her his sexy half-smile. "I ruined you for other men."

She let out a swoony sigh. "You wrecked me. No one even comes close to Marcus Shepard."

"Damn right."

"You're my forever love."

"Lexi, baby, you're mine."

"For God's sake," Ben chimed in, appearing out of nowhere. "Go home and get all this mushy stuff out of your system. It's nauseating."

Marcus narrowed his eyes. "Where's Missy?" That was Ben's fiancée.

"She'll be here soon," Ben growled. Suddenly he pulled his phone from his pocket, beaming as he answered it. "Hi, honey, how was shopping? Did you find a baptism outfit for Leo? Uh-huh. I can't wait to see…" Ben walked away, talking to his love, all sweetness. Leo was Missy's nephew.

Marcus and Lexi took one look at each other and cracked up.

"He's cranky without his woman," Marcus observed.

Lexi made a whip sound that had Marcus grinning.

Just then slow music started playing and Joe announced everyone should join him and Brandy in a dance. The high tables had been cleared near the bar area to make room.

Marcus took her hand. "Looks like they're playing our song."

She laughed and followed him the short distance to the dance floor. "You say every slow song is our song."

He pulled her close, holding her hand, his other hand resting lightly on her back. "That's because I love dancing with you. I'm so lucky I found you."

"Me too," she managed over the lump in her throat. "I can't believe I once thought you were the kind of man I could easily resist. You're way too tempting."

He leaned down to whisper, "You were just as tempting and I wanted in."

She smiled cheekily. "You sure got in."

He dipped his head and kissed her. "And I'm staying in."

After they'd put in their time—an hour plus of increasingly hotter dancing/foreplay—Marcus called it, cradling her jaw and kissing her. "Let's go back home to continue the celebration."

Which meant sex. "Celebrate, celebrate, that's all you want to do."

He winked. "You've given me a lot to celebrate."

"You give me a lot to celebrate too."

He stroked her cheek with his thumb, gazing into her eyes. "We're talking about the same thing, right? Or is this a touchy-feely talk?"

"You talk and I'll touchy-feely."

His dark eyes danced with amusement and tender love. The best kind of mushy, heart-squeezing, forever love. He grabbed her in a bear hug, lifting her off the ground. She couldn't stop smiling like a complete dope, crazy happy for her wonderful man.

And then they walked hand in hand out the door for their very own Happy Ending.

Dear Readers,

What the heck happened when Hailey went to Josh's place that caused a permanent rift between the pair? Did Josh really come to her rescue during her breakdown? Find out in Josh and Hailey's story, *An Inconvenient Plan*, book 10 in the Happy Endings Book Club series. Join the club and get your happy ending!

An Inconvenient Plan

Hailey Adams's strategy for a hugely successful wedding planning business is finally paying off, and now it's time to focus on her own happy ending. After a stinging rejection from her sexy frenemy, Josh Campbell, a prince falls into her lap. And he's a swoony, romantic contrast to the gruff bartender she can't seem to quit.

Josh's plan to keep his distance from Hailey is derailed when competition shows up in the form of a playboy prince. It's one damn inconvenience after another as Josh has to show up a prince, win over Hailey's rat-dog who hates him, and get Hailey to stop fighting with him long enough to see they belong together. Impossible woman!

Can these longtime frenemies let down their defenses in time to discover their own happy ending? Or will Hailey be swept off her feet by a fairy tale come true?

Sign up for my newsletter and never miss a new release! kyliegilmore.com/newsletter

ALSO BY KYLIE GILMORE

Unleashed Romance <<steamy romcoms with dogs!

Fetching (Book 1)

Dashing (Book 2)

Sporting (Book 3)

Toying (Book 4)

Blazing (Book 5)

Chasing (Book 6)

Daring (Book 7)

Leading (Book 8)

Racing (Book 9)

Loving (Book 10)

The Clover Park Series <<brothers who put family first!

The Opposite of Wild (Book 1)

Daisy Does It All (Book 2)

Bad Taste in Men (Book 3)

Kissing Santa (Book 4)

Restless Harmony (Book 5)

Not My Romeo (Book 6)

Rev Me Up (Book 7)

An Ambitious Engagement (Book 8)

Clutch Player (Book 9)

A Tempting Friendship (Book 10)

Clover Park Bride: Nico and Lily's Wedding

A Valentine's Day Gift (Book 11)

Maggie Meets Her Match (Book 12)

The Clover Park STUDS series <<hawt geeks who unleash into studs!

Almost Over It (Book 1)

Almost Married (Book 2)

Almost Fate (Book 3)

Almost in Love (Book 4)

Almost Romance (Book 5)

Almost Hitched (Book 6)

Happy Endings Book Club Series <<the Campbell family and a romance book club collide!

Hidden Hollywood (Book 1)

Inviting Trouble (Book 2)

So Revealing (Book 3)

Formal Arrangement (Book 4)

Bad Boy Done Wrong (Book 5)

Mess With Me (Book 6)

Resisting Fate (Book 7)

Chance of Romance (Book 8)

Wicked Flirt (Book 9)

An Inconvenient Plan (Book 10)

A Happy Endings Wedding (Book 11)

The Rourkes Series <<swoonworthy princes and kickass princesses!

Royal Catch (Book 1)

Royal Hottie (Book 2)

Royal Darling (Book 3)

Royal Charmer (Book 4)

Royal Player (Book 5)

Royal Shark (Book 6)

Rogue Prince (Book 7)

Rogue Gentleman (Book 8)

Rogue Rascal (Book 9)

Rogue Angel (Book 10)

Rogue Devil (Book 11)

Rogue Beast (Book 12)

Check out my website for the most up-to-date list of my books:
kyliegilmore.com/books

ABOUT THE AUTHOR

Kylie Gilmore is the *USA Today* bestselling author of the Unleashed Romance series, the Rourkes series, the Happy Endings Book Club series, the Clover Park series, and the Clover Park STUDS series. She writes humorous romance that makes you laugh, cry, and reach for a cold glass of water.

Kylie lives in New York with her family, two cats, and a nutso dog. When she's not writing, reading hot romance, or dutifully taking notes at writing conferences, you can find her flexing her muscles all the way to the high cabinet for her secret chocolate stash.

Sign up for Kylie's Newsletter and get a FREE book! kyliegilmore.com/newsletter

For text alerts on Kylie's new releases, text KYLIE to the number (888) 707-3025. (US only)

For more fun stuff check out Kylie's website https://www.kyliegilmore.com.

Thanks for reading *Wicked Flirt*. I hope you enjoyed it. Would you like to know about new releases? You can sign up for my new release email list at kyliegilmore.com/newsletter. I promise not to clog your inbox! Only new release info, sales, and some fun giveaways.

I love to hear from readers! You can find me at:
    kyliegilmore.com
    Instagram.com/kyliegilmore
    Facebook.com/KylieGilmoreToo
    Twitter @KylieGilmoreToo

If you liked Marcus and Lexi's story, please leave a review on your favorite retailer's website or Goodreads. Thank you.